Second Edition – May 2021

*Dedicated to everyone afflicted by spam emails,
a silent crime against your choice.*

Introduction

You will notice this paperback is not like your normal novel, it is a screenplay. The story and characters are similar to a novel but written in the industry format required when making a film. This is why the font (courier) and page format as like they are; it has been written using an industry standard script writing software. It is an easy read once you come to terms with the layout and format and it should be a lot quicker to read than the equivalent story in a standard fiction book. As a rule of thumb, one page of script roughly represents one minute of screen time. Although not a perfect rule, it is used by producers and directors to schedule the actual shooting of the film.

Who should read this? People who want to be scriptwriters or people studying film and require an understand of how a script looks and works. This particular book has been given to all the actors, crew and investors in the film 'Chocolate Potato' for them to work through making the film, which is why the last three pages are for their notes while working on the film.

We live in a fast world where time is always too short. Reading a script is a lot quicker than reading a book, so there is a new wave of interesting in reading a script to save time. The story and characters are no different than a novel version of the story, the only bit missing is the colour and vision. This is the job of the director but also the job of the reader to construct the scenes and images in their own mind. Some people also read screenplays before they see the film to compare how the script is designed and delivered to the silver screen. Whatever your reason for reading this screenplay, I hope you laugh out loud as you go through the bizarre journey the characters take.

This screenplay is the first of the 'Dark Journey Series' being published by H12 Media (h12.com). Watch out for future releases.

'Chocolate Potato'

By

Neil O'Neil

Original Screenplay
'A Raunchy Modern British Farce'
(Locked Script)

Neil O'Neil
Neil@screenplays.co.uk
mob: +44-7973-662021
www.screenplays.co.uk
@UKScreenplays

1   EXT. LONDON SUBURBIA - DAY

        Leafy suburb. Rain drenches terrace houses.

        POSTMAN, grey beard, turban, approaches gate. Stops. Faces
        Yorkshire Terrier having a dump in front garden.

        Dog GROWLS, bares teeth. Postie hesitates. Dog BARKS. He
        THROWS mail bundle toward step. It bounces off, knocks
        full milk bottle -- SMASH. Dog runs to the spill; LAPS.

        MISS FRANKLIN, red lipstick, buxom, curlers, skimpy
        dressing gown, comes out.

                         MISS FRANKLIN
                  Spicy! You bad dog.

        Shakes sharpened finger at dog; who hunkers down.

        Postie now next door, smiles. Scolded dog glares at
        postie, who sticks out his tongue.

        Miss Franklin bends to pick up post, displays tight red
        thong, very hairy arse crack. Postie winces, pushes single
        letter into letterbox, it BITES shut as the letter....

2   INT. JOEL'S HOUSE - CONTINUOUS - DAY

         ....floats through, onto mat, just misses the cat, who
        SPRINGS up stairs, to bedroom, under a double bed.

        SNORING above. A foot hangs over the edge.

        Ankle belongs to SALLY, 30, fit, blond. She GRABS a
        thermometer from bedside table; slides it under duvet,
        waits.

        The Arsenal adorned bedside clock CLICKS to 08:15.

        JOEL, 32, scruffy hair, beard; source of the SNORING.

        Sally removes thermometer from between her legs. READS.
        Triumphantly rips off the duvet. NAKED, straddles him.

                         SALLY
                  Come on big boy, time to sow
                  seed.

        Joel struggles to open his eyes; zero interest in sex.

                         JOEL
                  Do I have to?

                         SALLY
                  I'm ovulating so yes. Besides
                  you're obviously keen, I'm
                  sitting on a huge stiffy.

                                              (CONTINUED)

                         JOEL
               That's cos I need a piss. What
               time is it?

                         SALLY
               Time you showed interest in your
               wife. Don't you want a family?

Undeterred Sally continues to pump.

                         JOEL
               Wake me up when you've finished.

                         SALLY
               Most men would love free sex. The
               milkman asks for sex every
               morning when you've gone.

Joel too tired to register a smile.

                         JOEL
               Most men have more than four
               hours sleep.

                         SALLY
               That's your fault for coming home
               late. Once you've made a donation
               you can go back to sleep.

Sally pumps harder.

                         JOEL
               This is like rape.

She concentrates. Reluctantly Joel puts hands on her
waist; adjusts rhythm, angle of her hips. Then ORGASM.
She's in the final sprint. The clock clicks 08:18.

                         JOEL
               Bloody hell I'm late.

He goes to get up. She pushes him back down.

                         SALLY
               You'll wait til I've finished. I
               grin and bare it when you're on
               top.

He tries to stifle a yawn.

                         SALLY
               You could at least pretend you
               enjoy fucking me.

Eyes closed, he tweaks her nipples; a feeble effort.

3   INT. JOEL'S HOUSE - BEDROOM - DAY

Joel dresses. Sally's on her back; legs in the air.

                    JOEL
          Why you lying like that?

                    SALLY
          I don't want it to dribble out.

                    JOEL
          Can't you be normal? It'll happen
          when it's meant to.

                    SALLY
          You've been saying that for 12
          months. Don't you want a baby?

He stops dressing; sits next to her. Softens.

                    JOEL
          You know I do. I think you'll
          make a great mum.

                    SALLY
          So why don't you show more
          initiative?

                    JOEL
          I often want it at night but you
          have a headache or are asleep.

                    SALLY
          I've never stopped you.

                    JOEL
          That's like necrophilia. Women
          say they can multi-task, so why
          can't they do headache AND sex?

Sally sits up, punches his arm.

                    SALLY
          You cheeky bugger!

Noticing her legs are down, she quickly sticks them back
up. Joel gently kisses her.

                    JOEL
          You know I love you.

                    SALLY
          How long do you think I should
          lie like this?

                                                  (CONTINUED)

                    JOEL
          Until the milkman gets here. He
          can give you another pint.

She throws a pillow at him as he waves goodbye.

4   EXT. LONDON SUBURBIA - MORNING

        It's raining hard as Joel leaves home.

        Next door SPICY locked out, drenched, miserable.

        Joel pulls jacket over head and trots down the street.

        Huge puddle in road, fast car approaching. Driver takes
        aim. Joel steps back. Tsunami misses him; laughing he
        fingers the driver.

                    JOEL
          Missed me you smart arse!

        He turns, another car runs through puddle - drenched!

                    JOEL
              Shit!

5   INT. JOEL'S HOUSE - BATHROOM - DAY

        Sally on toilet, speaker phone; skims magazine.

                    SALLY
              We are so out of sync. He wants
              sex at night when I'm tired and I
              want it in the morning when he
              wants to sleep.

                    GILL (V.O)
              Have you tried to make a romantic
              meal and seduce him?

                    SALLY
              We're too familiar for that. He
              would be suspicious; as if I was
              having an affair.

                    GILL (V.O)
              Well it is your turn.

                    SALLY
              Less said about that the better.
              I don't think he'll do that
              again.

        Sally rips a huge FART, both burst into hysterics.

                                              (CONTINUED)

                         GILL (V.O)
               Did you have a curry last night?

                         SALLY
               No. A bottle of red, a bag of
               Nobbies nuts and fell asleep
               watching Suits.

                         GILL (V.O)
               Where was Joel?

                         SALLY
               Went to the bloody Arsenal and a
               piss-up afterwards. Got back
               silly o'clock.

                         GILL (V.O)
               Why don't we do lunch, hit the
               salon and then a night out?

                         SALLY
               I can't. I got to send some
               designs to IKEA by 2pm.

                         GILL (V.O)
               Well if things change I'm having
               a sickie today, so totally free.

                         SALLY
               Another one? You'll get the sack.

                         GILL (V.O)
               Unlikely, I'm screwing the boss.

                         SALLY
               You bugger. Anyway, got to go.
               Call you soon. Laters.

                         GILL (V.O)
               Bye Sal.

6   INT. SCHOOL - STAFF TOILETS - DAY

     Joel in underpants, holds wet trousers to hand dryer. BILL
     FOX, 37, tall, rugged, walks in.

                         BILL
               Pissed yourself again?

                         JOEL
               Attacked by a bloody puddle.

                         BILL
               Just pissed then.

                                                        (CONTINUED)

                         JOEL
          No it was this morning, not last
          night.

                         BILL
          What? Drinking in the morning
          now?

                         JOEL
          Fuck off Bill.

Bill takes a piss.

                         BILL
          We still playing squash today?

                         JOEL
          Of course.

Joel starts to put trousers on. School bell BLURTS. Joel
on one leg, poised to put other leg into trousers. Bill
opens door, gives Joel a slight shove. Joel loses balance;
stumbles into the middle of the school corridor.

Miss Spencer, 28, straight laced, passes as Joel tumbles
out, trousers down, y-fronts on display.

                         MISS SPENCER
          Mr Hancock. Make yourself decent!

Bill walks out, pulls his zip up.

                         BILL
          Same again tomorrow morning Joel?

Passing boys giggle. Miss Spencer turns crimson.

7   INT. SCHOOL - OUTSIDE CLASSROOM - DAY

     Joel late, dusts himself, deep breath. Enters.

8   INT. SCHOOL - INSIDE CLASSROOM - DAY

     Boys stand as he enters.

                         JOEL
          Morning boys. Please sit down.

                         CLASSROOM
          Good morning Mr. Hancock.

     He picks up large history book from desk.

                                                   (CONTINUED)

                         JOEL
               Right. Today, let's do Stalin.

There's an audible groan.

                         JOEL
               What's the matter with Stalin?
               Elmer why did you groan?

                         ELMER
               Sir we've been doing the second
               world war all term. It's boring.
               We know who won.

Ripples of laughter.

                         PATTERSON
               Sir, history's boring. Is there
               anything in history that's cool?

Joel looks out the window. A parent pushes a pram.

                         JONES
               Tell us something that few people
               know. Like a secret from history.

                         JOEL
               Right. I've got a deal for you.

They lean forward in anticipation.

                         JOEL (CONT'D)
               I'll tell you a little known
               secret from history and then back
               to the boring curriculum. Agreed?

Unanimous YES from class.

                         JOEL
               OK. Few people know that the day
               Germany invaded Poland, causing
               the outbreak of the second world
               war, was the same day Russia
               invaded Poland. However no
               sanctions were taken against
               Russia, only against Germany.

                         PATTERSON
               No way Sir.

                         JOEL
               Yes way Patterson.

                         SADLER
               So why didn't we punish the
               Russians?

                         JOEL
               Fear of the Ruskies. Hitler was a
               short arse and Germany was a
               smaller country. We thought we
               could kick his ass.

                         ELMER
               Are you shitting us Sir?

                         JOEL
               Not at all. So now you know how
               sneaky the Commies are, lets talk
               about Stalin.

Joel pleased with his victory, enthusiastically spins
towards the blackboard. The manoeuvre is a spectacular
fail, he spills across the floor, twisting his ankle. The
boys laugh, then realise he's hurt.

9   INT. JOEL'S HOUSE - LIVING ROOM - DAY

Sally, in dressing gown and PJ's, turns on laptop -- blue
screen of death!

                         SALLY
               Shit!

She moves to Joel's desk, loaded with battle scarred
exercise books. Turns on his computer -- the wallpaper's
bright red, Arsenal football club.

                         SALLY
               Bloody typical. He wouldn't think
               to have me as his wallpaper.

Screen prompts for password -- she spells out as types.

                         SALLY
               w-e-n-g-e-r.

Computer logs on.

                         SALLY
               How predictable Joel. Do I really
               want you to father my child?

She starts new email.

                         SALLY (V.O.)
               Dear Gill. Don't delete this
               email it's from me, Sally, not
               Joel. My laptop is fucked so I am
               using his computer. I've booked
               mum's cottage for next weekend; a
               girlie weekend. Haven't told Joel
               yet but as I'll have stopped
                         (MORE)

                                                      (CONTINUED)

                              SALLY (V.O.) (cont'd)
                    ovulating he's not much use. I
                    need a few days away. Who knows,
                    he may even miss me.

She presses send. Sips coffee. DING. An email comes into
Joel's mailbox.

EMAIL Subject: 'Another blowjob tonight Joel?'

Staring in disbelief she opens it.

                              SALLY (V.O.)
                    Hi Joel. I really enjoyed giving
                    you a blowjob after school last
                    night. I can't believe your wife
                    doesn't like sucking dick. Anyway
                    my friend Sharon wants to come
                    and watch me do it tonight. She
                    may even want some herself. As
                    you haven't got a car, we can use
                    mine again. Amy xx.

RAGE! She TOTALS desk. Framed Arsenal picture CRASHES to
floor.

Seething, she goes under sink - retrieves pot of WHITE
PAINT, paintbrush, Stanley knife. She THUNDERS upstairs to
his closet, paints all clothes; empties whole pot. Shreds
shirts with Stanley knife. Back to laptop - new email.

                              SALLY (V.O.)
                    Gill. Fuck the weekend. I can't
                    wait. I am coming over there now.
                    The wanker has been cheating on
                    me again. Make up the spare bed.

Sally prints Amy's email; then paints keyboard and screen.

10   INT. SCHOOL - METALWORK ROOM - DAY

Joel hobbles in -- one shoe off, ankle bandaged.

Bill works at the furnace, heats metal, turns to see Joel.

                              BILL
                    You'll do anything to get out of
                    squash.

                              JOEL
                    Sorry mate. Can barely walk.

                              BILL
                    So whose arse you kick? Elmer's?

                    JOEL
          Not that much fun. I fell down.

                    BILL
          Sure you're not drinking?

Joel ignores him.

                    JOEL
          Miss Spencer says it's only
          twisted. She bandaged it for me.

                    BILL
          I'm beginning to think there's
          something between you two.

Bill grabs WHITE HOT metal from furnace, PUSHES it towards
Joel's face -- then BRANDS a leather hide on work bench --
it HISSES as hot metal burns into it.

                    JOEL
          What the fuck? You could've had
          my eye out.

                    BILL
          Trust me. I know what I'm doing.

Joel watches the acrid smoke rise from the leather.

                    JOEL
          Are you sure?

                    BILL
          I bought Sam a leather saddle and
          riding boots for her birthday and
          now I'm branding them with her
          name. What you think?

Lifts branding iron, neatly burnt into leather - SAM. Joel
STARES blankly.

                    BILL (CONT'D)
          You don't seem impressed.

                    JOEL
          It's not that.

                    BILL
          What then?

                    JOEL
          You and Sam seem so happy.

                    BILL
          And the problem is?

                                              (CONTINUED)

                    JOEL
          I just wish me and Sal were.

                    BILL
          I thought you're nuts about her?

                    JOEL
          I am. But she's getting impatient
          about starting a family.

                    BILL
          Don't you want kids?

                    JOEL
          Of course I do but I can't just
          perform at the drop of a hat.

                    BILL
          Something wrong with the old
          pecker then?

                    JOEL
          Not at all. It works very well.
          But this morning she nearly raped
          me because she's ovulating.

                    BILL
          You lucky bugger. Waking up to a
          horny bitch.

                    JOEL
          Well I didn't enjoy it. I don't
          think she got much out of it.

                    BILL
          I thought you said she was a
          fabulous shag.

                    JOEL
          I told you that?

                    BILL
          You were wrecked at the time.

Joel zones out looking at branded leather.

                    BILL (CONT'D)
          Well is she?

                    JOEL
          Is she what?

                    BILL
          A fabulous shag?

                         JOEL
               None of your business.

                         BILL
               We could swap car keys.

                         JOEL
               I ain't got a car.

                         BILL
               It's a euphemism for wife
               swapping. Then I could tell you
               if it's true.

                         JOEL
               If what's true?

                         BILL
               If she's a great shag.

                         JOEL
               Fuck off Bill

Joel hobbles off. Bill shouts after him.

                         BILL
               I'll throw in Sam's horse to make
               a threesome. Huge dick.

School bell RINGS. Pupils file into classroom.

11   INT. SCHOOL TEACHERS STAFF ROOM - DAY

Joel hobbles into staff room. Old Fletcher asleep on sofa,
dribbles; Miss Spencer drinks tea, reads 'Buddhism Today'.
Joel sits next to Miss Spencer.

                         JOEL
               Thank you for attending to my
               ankle.

Suddenly Sally BURSTS in carrying a bulging ASDA bag.

                         SALLY
               You slime bag!

He tries to rise. She pushes him back down. Fletcher
wakes, sees Sally in full flight, snoozes again.

                         SALLY
               You cheating bastard!

                         JOEL
               What you on about? I've done
               nothing.

                                              (CONTINUED)

                         SALLY
               So who gave you a blow job last
               night?

Miss Spencer looks up in horror. Sally glares at her.

                         MISS SPENCER
               It wasn't me!

                         JOEL
               Have you lost your mind?

Sally retrieves printout of email.

                         SALLY
               So what's this then?

Thrusts at him. His eyes widen. She scans bandage.

                         JOEL
               I've no idea what this is.

                         SALLY
               You're a liar. It explains why
               you were late last night and
               didn't want sex this morning.

Old Fletcher wakes at 'sex'. Miss Spencer raises hand to
her mouth, leaves, giving Sally a wide berth.

                         FLETCHER
               Can I watch?

Sally unintentionally flashes cleavage in Fletcher's face.

                         SALLY
                    (at Flecther)
               Go back to sleep old man.
                    (back to Joel)
               After last time I said you were
               on your last chance. I meant it.
               We're through!

Empties ASDA bag on table -- house keys, wedding ring,
other romantic memorabilia tumble out. Joel's
speechless. With a swift lunge Sally slaps his face.

                         SALLY
               You're out of my life. For good.
               You'll be hearing from my lawyer
               about a divorce.

Sally heads to the door, as Bill enters.

                         BILL
               Hi Sally.

                                              (CONTINUED)

                    SALLY
          Fuck off Bill.

Sally storms out. Bill turns to Joel.

                    BILL
          Was that about the car keys or
          the horse?

                    JOEL
          She wants a divorce.

                    BILL
          There goes that fabulous shag.

Old Fletcher, half asleep, looks up again.

                    FLETCHER
          Can I watch?

12   INT. SCHOOL - METALWORK ROOM - DAY

        Bill reads email. Joel looks at branding iron.

                    BILL
          I kinda guessed the mood you came
          in this morning you can't have
          had your dick sucked last night.

                    JOEL
          Is that all you think about?

                    BILL
          What else is there? How many
          blowjobs do you think I'm getting
          for branding all this leather?

                    JOEL
          What about my marriage? What
          about the family we're planning?
          What the fuck do I do now?

                    BILL
          If you know nothing about this
          then either someone's winding you
          up or it's been sent in error.

                    JOEL
          It's addressed to me, knows I am
          a teacher, that I am married,
          that Sally doesn't like giving
          blowjobs and that I don't drive.
          There is nothing random about it.
          This email is to me.

                                              (CONTINUED)

                         BILL
          Have you tried replying to it?

                         JOEL
          And say what? Thanks for ruining
          my life; I may as well now take
          that blowjob. Thank fucking you.

                         BILL
          No you idiot. If you reply you
          might find out who it's actually
          from and then we can erase them.

                         JOEL
          I suppose that makes some sense.
          Except the erasing them bit.

13   INT. GILL'S FLAT - HAMMERSMITH - DAY

        Sally's CRYING, Gill comforts her. Two empty wine glasses,
        full ashtray on table.

                         SALLY
          How could he do this? I thought
          he loved me.

                         GILL
          Men only think with their dicks.

                         SALLY
          He told this slag Amy that I
          don't like giving blowjobs.

                         GILL
          I don't like giving blowjobs.

                         SALLY
          Really? I thought it was just me.

                         GILL
          Who wants to suck something
          that's been pissed out of? No
          woman likes to give a blowjob.

                         SALLY
          Well Amy and Sharon do!

        Sally bursts into tears again.

                         GILL
          Tell you what. Go have a bath.
          Relax. I'll cook us some tea and
          tonight let's hit the town and
          get wasted.

                         SALLY
               Thanks Gill, you're a great mate.

They embrace.

14   EXT. JOEL'S HOUSE - NIGHT

Miss Franklin, dressed like a trollop, watches her dog
take a dump. Bill's Rover 90 pulls up. Joel hobbles out on
crutches -- Miss Franklin waves.

                         MISS FRANKLIN
               Hi Joel darling. What have you
               done to your foot?

                         BILL
               He kicked a pupil.

                         MISS FRANKLIN
               Is that true Joel?

Joel shakes his head, struggles with keys. Bill blatantly
ogles her.

                         MISS FRANKLIN (CONT'D)
               Who's your nice friend.

Bill holds his hand out, eyes her cleavage.

                         BILL
               Bill Fox. Amateur gynecologist.

Miss Franklin shakes, then touches the back of her hair.

                         MISS FRANKLIN
               You're a naughty boy.

Joel quickly opens the door, drags Bill in.

                         JOEL
               Are you totally mad? She's the
               local bike.

                         BILL
               She's gagging for it. Once you
               ride a bike you never forget.

                         JOEL
               You've obvious never rode a penny
               farthing.

                         BILL
               Eh?

Joel is first to enter the study.

                                              (CONTINUED)

                        JOEL
             Oh shit!

It's destroyed. Painted on wall; LIAR - BASTARD - CHEAT.

                        JOEL
             Oh no!

                        BILL
             She's a fucking nutter. Where's
             the bathroom? I need a piss.

Joel points upstairs; hobbles to display cabinet - Arsenal
pictures, rosettes, programs
sliced to shreds.

                        BILL (O.S)
             Bloody hell. She's a bunny
             boiler.

Joel hobbles to stairs; Bill holds a suit; it drips paint.

15   INT. GILL'S FLAT - HAMMERSMITH - NIGHT

The girls put make-up on. Gill, bra, pants, fishnets, in
front of double mirror with tacky light bulb surround.

                        GILL
             A few G and T's and you'll feel
             better.

                        SALLY
             I didn't think it would hit me so
             hard. I've always relied on him
             to pay the mortgage and things.

                        GILL
             Well there's the first payout;
             force him to sell the house and
             you get half the money.

                        SALLY
             He had the house before we met.

                        GILL
             You said you wanted to take him
             to the cleaners. It's a shame you
             didn't have kids, you could
             really stitch him up.

Sally stops mid flow; ready to burst into tears.

                        GILL
             I'm sorry. I know how much you
             want kids. Anyway there's more
             sperm in the sea and tonight
             we're going fishing.

                                              (CONTINUED)

                    SALLY
          Is that why you're wearing
          fishnets?

Gill looks at her fishnet tights and laughs.

                    GILL
          That was funny Sal. See you're
          becoming your old self again.

Sally silent, tries not to cry.

16   INT. BILL'S HOUSE - NIGHT

Joel's having dinner with Bill, his wife, SAM, 38, dumpy;
and their daughter MAISIE, 10, precocious. Bill's plate's
empty. He looks around for more. Joel plays with his food.

                    MAISIE
          Mummy says your wife doesn't love
          you any more.

                    SAM
          Maisie. I didn't say that. I said
          they've had a little argument,
          like I have with daddy.

                    MAISIE
          So will daddy be going to jail
          next time you have an argument?

The adults look at each other confused.

                    BILL
          What do you mean Maisie?

                    MAISIE
          Well jail has come to us?

                    SAM
          Maisie his name is Joel, not
          jail.

They laugh; except Maisie, mad at being butt of joke.

                    MAISIE
          Well I think he smells. If I was
          his wife I would leave him.

                    SAM
          Maisie don't be so rude. He
          doesn't smell.

                    MAISIE
          He does. He smells of paint and
          his hands are white.

                                              (CONTINUED)

They look at Joel's hands, he drops them under the table.
Embarrassing silence.

                    JOEL
          Bill's going to help me sort
          things out online. Aren't you
          Bill?

                    BILL
          Er yes. We need to search Ebay
          for some Arsenal memorabilia.

                    SAM
          As long as you're not surfing for
          porn.

                    MAISIE
          Mummy what's porn?

Sam blushes, Joel helps her out.

                    JOEL
          It's a wooden chess piece.

                    MAISIE
          You smell!

                    BILL
          Let's go Joel the women are
          ganging up on us.

Maisie sticks her tongue out. Sam gets an old cloth and
white spirit from a drawer.

                    SAM
          Don't you dare make a mess.

Bill motions for Joel to follow with laptop in ASDA bag.

                    JOEL
          Thanks for dinner Sam. Bye Daisy.

                    MAISIE
          It's Maisie.

The girls watch, arms crossed as the guys leave the room.

17   INT. BILL'S HOUSE - NIGHT

Joel and Bill upstairs - small study. Laptop's open, dirty
cloth, white spirit bottle close by.

                    BILL
          What a mess. I'm amazed it still
          works.

                                              (CONTINUED)

                         JOEL
          So what should I write?

                         BILL
          Budge up.

Bill takes control. Typing FAST.

                         JOEL
          How come you know your way around
          a computer so well?

                         BILL
          Misspent childhood.

                         JOEL
          So why you teaching metalwork
          when you're such a computer whiz?

                         BILL
          It's a long story. (beat) Here's
          the bloody problem.

Bill types at lightening speed.

                         BILL (CONT'D)
          I replied to the email and it's
          been returned as a non-existent
          email address.

                         JOEL
          What's the point of that? Surely
          spam is sent in the hope of
          generating some income.

                         BILL
          It is and this one has installed
          an AOB.

                         JOEL
          What the fuck's an AOB? Any other
          business?

Bill excited, engrossed in the laptop.

                         BILL
          AOB stands for Ads by Object
          Browser. A piece of malware that
          opens loads of porn windows when
          you search for something.

                         JOEL
          That sounds juvenile. How do they
          make money from that? All I need
          to do is close the windows.

                    BILL
          That's the clever bit. Each time
          you close a window it registers a
          click on the porn site. Every
          click earns money, whether you
          look at the porn or not.

                    JOEL
          Bastards. How on earth do they
          charge me for that?

                    BILL
          You don't pay, the advertising
          company pays. Let's test it.

                    JOEL
          How on earth did this AOB get on
          my machine?

                    BILL
          You must have clicked on a link
          in that email.

                    JOEL
          I didn't. I've only just seen it.

Bill clicks on the offending email.

                    BILL
          Clever bastards. The email is
          signed by Amy. Her name is the
          link. Sally must have clicked it.

                    JOEL
          So Sally has infected my laptop
          with porn?

                    BILL
          Ironic eh? Let's search Google
          for Arsenal. Better not, there's
          an arse in it. Let's try BBC.

Bill types BBC into Google, porn windows pop up.

                    JOEL
          Fuck a duck. Look at that porn.

                    BILL
          Shall we? Wow! Look at that BBW.

Unnoticed, Sam has walked in behind them.

                    SAM
          No you don't! I leave you alone
          for a minute and you're looking
          at smutty porn sites.

Sam thumps Bill in the back.

                    BILL
          It's Sally's fault she put links
          to porn on Joel's laptop.

                    SAM
          Yeah right. And I am virgin.

                    JOEL
          It's complicated Sam.

                    SAM
          Shut up. You're a bad influence.
          I think it's time you left.

                    BILL
          I'll take you home Joel. I think
          it's the wrong time of the month.

                    SAM
          Fuck off Bill.

Sam storms out of the room - SLAMS door.

18   INT. BILL'S CAR - NIGHT

        Bill and Joel are in the car having left Bill's house.

                    JOEL
          How come you're so computer
          savvy?

                    BILL
          I'm bloody starving. Fancy an
          Indian?

                    JOEL
          We've just had dinner.

                    BILL
          Yeah and Sam put half my dinner
          on your plate. Which you hardly
          touched.

                    JOEL
          I got other things on my mind
          than food at moment.

                    BILL
          You can always watch.

                    JOEL
          Watch what?

                    BILL
          Me eating an Indian.

                         JOEL
               Only if you answer my question.

Bill looks at Joel -- can he trust him?

                         BILL
               OK. If you buy the Indian I'll
               tell you my secret.

                         JOEL
               Sounds ominous. You're on.

                         BILL
               What about the Shag Bag?

                         JOEL
               You back on porn again?

                         BILL
               No the restaurant on Riverside.

                         JOEL
               You mean the Shah Bagh.

                         BILL
               That's what I said. Shag Bag.

Bill elbows him -- matey gesture.

                         BILL (CONT'D)
               Hold on tight numb nuts, Bill's
               going to take you on an excellent
               adventure.

                         JOEL
               Can't wait. By the way what does
               BBW stand for?

                         BILL
               Big Breasted Women. Just like the
               horny Miss Franklin.

                         JOEL
               Thanks. I was starting to get my
               appetite back.

19   INT. BARBARELLA'S NIGHTCLUB - NIGHT

PUMPING LOUD DISCO MUSIC. Packed club. BUZZING.

Gill and Sally - line of shots in front of them.

Two suave guys next to them, pints in hand. Small crowd
gathered around. One guy counts down -- THREE - TWO - ONE.

Both girls knock back shots, grab the next, knock it back, then the next. Gill's first to put the last empty on the bar. Sally seconds behind. Crowd cheer and clap.

20   INT. BARBARELLA'S NIGHTCLUB - LATER - NIGHT

Music now BALLAD. Gill and a guy smooch -- hands grope.

Sally dances with other guy - not as close or gross. He leans forward, lightly kisses her lips. She kisses back.

21   INT. SHAH BAGH RESTAURANT - NIGHT

Bill and Joel eat poppadoms/chutney -- empty restaurant.

                    BILL
          You got your appetite back then.

                    JOEL
          If I'm paying for it I may as
          well eat something. So what's the
          big secret?

                    BILL
          Can I trust you Joel?

                    JOEL
          That's a stupid question.

                    BILL
          I'm serious. I haven't even told
          Sam this.

Joel nods seriously. Bill looks around.

                    BILL
          My name ain't Bill Fox.

                    JOEL
          Fuck! What is it?

                    BILL
          That's not important. Bill Fox is
          dead.

                    JOEL
          Oh Shit. Are you a murderer?

                    BILL
          No. No. Nothing like that. He
          died of a heart attack while
          hitch-hiking around Oz. I just
          took over his identity.

(CONTINUED)

                         JOEL
               What the hell for?

                         BILL
               I am getting to that numb nuts if
               you stop asking inane questions.

Joel gestures mouth 'zipping'.

                         BILL (CONT'D)
               I was on the run from the spooks.
               Nothing serious like terrorism. I
               was a hacker and broke into some
               important military listening
               stations. Posted the stuff on the
               Internet and it raised bloody
               hell.

                         JOEL
               Like wikileaks?

                         BILL
               I was years ahead of Assange. I
               managed to slip out of the
               country in the boot of a car of a
               hippy anti-establishment couple.

Joel astonished.

                         BILL (CONT'D)
               I think the police were using
               Interpol to find me, as I found
               wanted notices on the Police
               National Computer.

                         JOEL
               You broken into the PNC?

                         BILL
               Piece of piss.

                         JOEL
               Bloody hell. You're a dark horse.
               What happened?

                         BILL
               I spent 3 months in OZ with Bill
               Fox. He was an English orphan
               travelling the world looking for
               a place to settle. I was with him
               when he died; so had access to
               all his belongings and papers;
               before I buried him.

                         JOEL
               Shit a brick. Are you serious?

                                            (CONTINUED)

                              BILL
                    Deadly.

Bill finishes his beer and lets out a loud belch.

                              BILL (CONT'D)
                    Now I have a dull normal job that
                    has nothing to do with computers.
                    A normal family and home. I think
                    I am finally off their radar.

                              JOEL
                    Is that why you have no computer
                    at home?

                              BILL
                    Yep. It's too tempting. I can
                    break into any system. But
                    nowadays they put you inside for
                    good for doing that.

                              JOEL
                    Thanks for trusting me with that.

                              BILL
                    It's OK, I'll just kill you if
                    you tell anyone.

Waiter brings food on a trolley -- enough to feed four.

                              JOEL
                    Do you think we can eat all this?

                              BILL
                    Who gives a shit? You're paying.

22   INT. GILL'S FLAT - HAMMERSMITH - MORNING

Sally sleeps on the bed settee. Clothes strewn -- Knickers
on lampshade - bra over TV. Smudged make-up face.

She stirs, turns over, face to face with last nights guy.
COLIN CURTIS, 40, fit, ripped, awake watching her.

She recoils, pulls sheet tighter to cover her modesty.

                              COLIN
                    Good morning Bagpuss!

                              SALLY
                    What kind of greeting's that? And
                    what are you doing here?

                              COLIN
                    Two questions in one breath. I
                    guess you must be sober. Bagpuss,
                    is your favourite character.

                    SALLY
          Did I tell you that?

                    COLIN
          So much more. The reason I'm
          naked is because you ripped my
          clothes off demanding the use of
          my body to help you get even or
          something.

                    SALLY
          Did we. You know. Do anything?

                    COLIN
          Hardly. By the time you had
          completed your striptease you
          passed out in my arms.

                    SALLY
          So you didn't take advantage of
          me or anything?

                    COLIN
          Not at all.

                    SALLY
          You're not gay are you?

                    COLIN
          Nope. Far from it.

                    SALLY
          So if you didn't take advantage,
          why are you still here? Most guys
          just disappear in the morning.

                    COLIN
          Amazing as it sounds I find you
          hilarious and attractive. I
          wanted to meet you without the
          company of Mr Gordons.

                    SALLY
          Did I make a fool of myself?

                    COLIN
          Most certainly.

                    SALLY
          Oh Shit! How embarrassing was I?

                    COLIN
          Well the taxi driver knows your
          choice in underwear, how you like
          to go on top and that you hate
          blow jobs.

                    SALLY
          I am so sorry. I don't normally
          act like that. It's been a
          difficult few days.

                    COLIN
          Not a problem. No harm done and
          my virginity's still in tact.

                    SALLY
          You're a virgin?

                    COLIN
          Only last night.

Colin smirks, adjusts his tackle under the covers. Sally
lifts the cover, takes a peek. Impressed.

                    SALLY
          I still need some payback; does
          he want to make a contribution?

                    COLIN
          How could he refuse?

Colin leans over - passionately kisses Sally. She responds
-- in moments they're in passionate embrace. He mounts
her. Gill, peers through crack in the door, chooses her
moment, sneaks behind them - to the bathroom.

On her way back she looks at Colin's bare arse, pumping
away at Sally.

Back into bed alone. Lights cigarette, reads magazine.

We hear Sally's excitement rising.

                    GILL
          Lucky bitch!

23   INT. SCHOOL - METALWORK ROOM - DAY

Joel watches Bill working the furnace. Metal letters on
the bench next to his branding iron.

                    JOEL
          Didn't she like your handiwork?

                    BILL
          She loved it. As a peace offering
          I laid it out this morning on the
          kitchen table. Now she wants the
          name of the horse branded on
          everything as well.

                                              (CONTINUED)

                         JOEL
               What did she name the horse?

                         BILL
               Jumper.

                         JOEL
               That's a stupid name for a horse!

                         BILL
               I know, but apparently when she
               was small there was a horse in
               the back field called Juniper.
               She couldn't say Juniper so
               always called it Jumper.

Joel plays with the cold metal letters on the work bench.

                         JOEL
               You're really a romantic at
               heart.

Bill stokes coal in the furnace.

                         BILL
               She's nearly up to heat.

Joel re-arranges the letters to spell SPAMMER. Bill walks
over, sees him transfixed on the word he's made.

                         BILL
               Bloody hell mate. That email is
               fucking with your head.

                         JOEL
               Say what?

                         BILL
               I said Miss Spencer wants to give
               you head.

                         JOEL
               Oh fuck off Bill!

Joel storms out. Bill looks at the word SPAMMER.

24   INT. SCHOOL - CORRIDOR - CONTINUOUS - DAY

Joel SKULKS down the corridor, puts his coat on. Old
Fletcher going the other way, stops.

                         FLETCHER
               Mr. Perkins, do you know where I
               might find the headmaster?

                    JOEL
          Up my arse!

Joel rushes through the front doors as Miss Spencer walks
in -- They collide. She falls back. Her long dress flies
over her head - reveals skimpy red knickers, suspenders.
He offers to help her up, eyes glued to her sexy apparel.

                    JOEL
          I'm so sorry.

                    MISS SPENCER
          Don't touch me you cheating
          pervert.

Joel withdraws hand - scoots off muttering to himself.
Bill watches from his classroom window.

25   INT. GILL'S FLAT - HAMMERSMITH - DAY

Both girls on couch - drink coffee.

                    GILL
          It doesn't have to be a one night
          stand. He's loaded, did you see
          the Rolex?

                    SALLY
          One morning stand.

                    GILL
          If he was gentlemanly enough to
          wait until you were sober, then
          he might not be such a bastard.

                    SALLY
          How do I know it's not just a
          rebound thing?

                    GILL
          You don't, but where is the
          downside? He's a good lay and..

                    SALLY
          How do you know he's a good lay?

                    GILL
          Sally, you were coming like a
          steam train this morning and I
          think you arrived on more than
          one platform.

                    SALLY
          Was I that loud?

                                              (CONTINUED)

                         GILL
             You set the neighbour's dog off
             howling in sympathy.

                         SALLY
             I'm so sorry. Joel was never able
             to do that to me.

                         GILL
             No need to apologize, you needed
             it. Just promise me one thing?

                         SALLY
             Sure. Anything.

                         GILL
             If it doesn't work out, let me
             have a go at him. My boiler needs
             a good stoking.

Both burst into giggles.

26   INT. JOEL'S HOUSE - BEDROOM - NIGHT

     Joel sits on his bed, strokes the cat, in the dark, fully
     dressed, stares straight ahead, at nothing.

     Crackly radio from another room - Archers theme tune.

     Suddenly, iPhone on side table SCREECHES into life.

     DISPLAY - Bill Fox. Joel mutes call - lets it ring. He's
     in the ZONE - dark thoughts. TEXT MESSAGE from Bill.

     TEXT: Numb nuts, Miss Spencer wants her dignity back.
     Dirty bitch. Get your head out your arse. Got an idea.

     Joel turns the phone off, strokes purring cat.

27   INT. LANGAN'S BRASSERIE - NIGHT

     Sally SMILES - SIPS wine. Colin SCHMOOZES her.

                         COLIN
             I'm not going to propose if
             that's what's worrying you.

                         SALLY
             You can't anyway, I'm still
             married.

                         COLIN
             I know nothing about you other
             than you're a wounded wife. Do
             you work?

                                              (CONTINUED)

                    SALLY
          Yes. I'm a freelance designer.

                    COLIN
          What type of design?

                    SALLY
          I'm a graphic designer.

                    COLIN
          Can you design for websites?

                    SALLY
          Yes. Why?

                    COLIN
          I own a web hosting company and
          could do with a good designer.

                    SALLY
          Does that mean I would be working
          under you?

                    COLIN
          I may let you go on top a few
          times.

He SMILES - they LAUGH. Glasses CLINK!

28   INT. SCHOOL - CLASSROOM - DAY

      Joel's absent -- Old Fletcher tries to cover.

                    ELMER
          Sir is it true Mr Hancock fancies
          Miss Spencer?

                    FLETCHER
          Who's Mr. Hancock?

                    JONES
          Our normal history teacher.

                    FLETCHER
          I understand Mr. Hancock is
          feeling unwell.

                    SADLER
          Sure he's not feeling Miss
          Spencer?

      Titters.

                    FLETCHER
          Calm down boys. I know your
          hormones are raging, but let's
                    (MORE)

                                              (CONTINUED)

                         FLETCHER (cont'd)
               try to do some work. Let's see if
               we can get through this lesson
               without me having to spank you.

Fletcher's attempt at a joke fails.

                         FURBER
               Sir, can we spank the monkey?

Room erupts - boys pelt Furber with balls of screwed-up
paper - cacophony of 'WANKER'. Room dissolves to chaos.
Nobody notices the classroom door open.

                         BILL
               Sit the fuck down and shut the
               fuck up! Before I dismember
               someone!

Total silence. Boys shrivel into their seats.

                         BILL
               Where's Joel?

                         FLETCHER
               Joel who?

                         BILL
               Joel Hancock. The real history
               teacher.

                         FLETCHER
               Oh him. Got the measles. Doctor's
               note for a week.

                         BILL
               Shit.

                         PATTERSON
               You shouldn't swear in the
               classroom Sir.

                         BILL
               And you shouldn't breathe.

Patterson shrinks. Bill addresses the class.

                         BILL
               Right boys. I'm in the metalwork
               room next door and if I hear a
               bleat out of any of you while Mr
               Fletcher stands in, I'll stand on
               you. CLEAR?

A few mumbles.

                                              (CONTINUED)

                        BILL
            I SAID CLEAR?

                        CLASS
            Yes Mr Fox.

                        BILL
            Clear enough Mr Fletcher?

                        FLETCHER
            Clear as mud. Thank you.

Leaving, Bill points finger round the room. A warning.

29   EXT. JOEL'S HOUSE - DAY

        Bill knocks on door. No reply. Knocks louder. BBW from
        next door comes out.

                        MISS FRANKLIN
            I think he's asleep darling. He
            didn't go to work this morning.

                        BILL
            Are you sure he's not dead?

                        MISS FRANKLIN
            He wasn't dead at 4 this morning

                        BILL
            How do you know?

30   INT. JOEL'S HOUSE - CONTINUOUS - DAY

        A curtain moves -- Joel looks out.

        JOEL'S POV: SEES BILL SPEAKING WITH MISS FRANKLIN.

31   EXT. FRANKLIN'S GARDEN - LONDON - DAY

        Bill walks towards Miss Franklin.

                        MISS FRANKLIN
            I was doing some research on TV,
            when I saw the bathroom light
            come on. I know it couldn't be
            Sally, she's left him. Poor dear.

                        BILL
            What research can you do on TV at
            4 in the morning?

                                            (CONTINUED)

                         MISS FRANKLIN
               Babestation.

                         BILL
               Babestation?

                         MISS FRANKLIN
               Yes, I was thinking of applying
               for it.

                         BILL
               As a BBW?

                         MISS FRANKLIN
               You know about that?

                         BILL
               Oh yes. I know a lot about that.

                         MISS FRANKLIN
               Do you think I would fit?

Bill blatantly looks at her cleavage.

                         BILL
               Only on wide screen.

                         MISS FRANKLIN
               Cheeky boy. Would you like a cup
               of tea?

Front door opens -- Joel, dishevelled, pops his head out.

                         JOEL
               Bill. Come on in.

                         BILL
               Give me ten minutes mate?

                         JOEL
               No. NOW.

Bill turns back to Miss Franklin.

                         BILL
               Got to go; but I'll take a
               rain-check on that.

                         MISS FRANKLIN
               You don't need to wait until it's
               raining darling.

Bill disappears into Joel's house. Miss Franklin struts.

32   INT. JOEL'S HOUSE - HALLWAY - DAY

Joel closes the door.

                    BILL
          I was in there mate.

                    JOEL
          You're in here now. How on Earth
          can you be so blatant? I make
          every effort to avoid her.

                    BILL
          How can you not want to jingle
          those bells?

                    JOEL
          You're insane. What about Sam?

                    BILL
          Her tits are small. Can't really
          do much with them.

                    JOEL
          No. What if she found out?

                    BILL
          Well I'm not going to tell her.
          Got a beer? I'm parched.

Bill strides to the fridge, extracts cold beer, SLUGS,
BELCHES, sits down grinning like a Cheshire cat.

                    JOEL
          You're intolerable.

Joel settles across from Bill.

                    JOEL (CONT'D)
          I'm not really in the mood for
          company at the moment.

                    BILL
          Apparently you've got the
          measles.

                    JOEL
          I haven't got measles.

                    BILL
          So what have you got?

                    JOEL
          Why should I have anything?

(CONTINUED)

                         BILL
          Because you didn't turn up today
          and you acted like a knob
          yesterday.

                         JOEL
          What knocking Miss Spencer over?
          That was an accident.

                         BILL
          Not that. In fact that was a high
          point of the day, did you see..

                         JOEL
          Yes Bill I know you're a pervert.
          But that doesn't make me a knob.

                         BILL
          You're a knob 'cos you wouldn't
          answer the phone or my texts. I'm
          supposed to be your mate.

                         JOEL
          I need space.

                         BILL
          Space? Do you think you're the
          first man to lose a woman?

                         JOEL
          Sally's not just a woman, she's
          my wife.

                         BILL
          So now you need a new plan.

Joel leans forward and gets in Bill's face.

                         JOEL
          Why the fuck do I need a new plan
          Bill? I'm happy with the old plan
          and it was all going well until
          some shit sent that crazy email.

                         BILL
          You can't turn back time. Shit
          happens.

                         JOEL
          Just because you take shit from
          everyone, doesn't mean I have to.

Awkward silence.

                         JOEL (CONT'D)
          I'm sorry. That was mean. I told
          you I wasn't good company.

                                              (CONTINUED)

More silence.

                    BILL
          Hypothetically speaking if you
          could do anything, how do you
          think you could win Sally back?

                    JOEL
          If I can prove that email was a
          fake, she might forgive me.

                    BILL
          They obviously got your details
          from your Facebook page.

                    JOEL
          Is it possible to find the
          spammer?

                    BILL
          He could be anywhere!

                    JOEL
          But how possible is it?

                    BILL
          Technically it can be done. The
          police do it to find paedophiles.

                    JOEL
          Could you do it?

                    BILL
          I could. But what then? He's not
          going to fess up to it.

                    JOEL
          With a gun to his head he might?

                    BILL
          Now you're being silly. As if
          you've got a gun.

Joel slowly brings a small gun from his dressing gown
pocket. Bill jumps back in shock.

                    BILL
          What the fuck? Where did you get
          that?

                    JOEL
          Brixton.

                    BILL
          What you walked down Brixton High
          Street and just shouted out.
          'Anyone got a gun I could have'?

                                              (CONTINUED)

                    JOEL
          You ain't the only one who's lead
          a misspent youth. Leroy has
          contacts wiv da hood.

                    BILL
          Who the fuck is Leroy?

                    JOEL
          Monster Gooners fan. It only cost
          300 quid.

                    BILL
          Is it loaded?

                    JOEL
          I got 6 bullets with it. Not sure
          who they're for yet, but I'm
          saving one for me.

                    BILL
          Now you're talking stupid.

Joel breaks down.

                    JOEL
          I don't want to live without her.
          No one knows me like she does.
          Bill, I don't know what to do.

Joel uncontrollably sobs. Bill speechless, slugs beer.

33   INT. JOEL'S LIVING ROOM - 1 HOUR LATER - DAY

Bill and Joel drink coffee, look at the gun on the table.

                    BILL
          If I was a real mate I'd report
          this to the police - get you
          locked up for your own safety.

                    JOEL
          So why don't you?

                    BILL
          'Cos this is so cool. I never
          thought you had this in you.

                    JOEL
          Have you got a camera?

                    BILL
          I got one on my phone. You want
          to Facebook your gun?

                                              (CONTINUED)

                         JOEL
               No a proper video camera. To
               video the hackers confession when
               we find him.

                         BILL
               Yeah. I bought one for the hols
               last year, why? (light bulb
               moment) I could record a
               Babestation audition.

                         JOEL
               Is that all you ever think about?

                         BILL
               It's better than thinking of
               suicide.

Bill releases the magazine -- weighs it in his hand.

                         BILL
               OK I'll help you, but only if you
               promise me that if this goes tits
               up you don't do something stupid
               like top yourself.

                         JOEL
               Agreed. Thanks Bill, you're my
               only hope.

                         BILL
               Don't mention it. Meet me at
               Kings Cross station tomorrow
               morning at 5am, bring your laptop
               and leave your mobile phone at
               home. Capich?

                         JOEL
               You what?

                         BILL
               This is now a black op and I'm
               mission commander. Do you want to
               find the spammer?

                         JOEL
               Well, Yes.

                         BILL
               Good. Now get some rest.

                         JOEL
               What you going to do?

                         BILL
               I got a Babestation interview.

                          JOEL
                Where?

                          BILL
                That's classified soldier. Need
                to know basis only.

Bill throws a mock salute, leaves.

34   INT. STARBUCKS - DAY

Gill and Sally share a muffin with their lattes.

                          SALLY
                He wants me to work for him.

                          GILL
                Go for it girl! I'll support you
                all the way.

                          SALLY
                Thanks Gill. If it wasn't for you
                I'd probably have sulked a while,
                then gone back to the bastard.

                          GILL
                He's going to regret ever
                cheating on you.

Both sip their coffee. Sally tries a smile.

35   INT. KINGS CROSS STATION - MORNING

Joel and Bill enter an empty first class carriage. Joel
holding coffees, Bill with a WH Smith's bag.

                          JOEL
                OK Mr Bond. Why have I bought 1st
                class day returns to Edinburgh
                and left my mobile at home?

                          BILL
                Mobile phones are GPS monitoring
                devices. Leaving it at home gives
                you an alibi. You can stick with
                your measles story and say you
                were at home the whole time.

                          JOEL
                I don't have measles. The whole
                time for what? What are you
                planning in Edinburgh? Does the
                spammer live there?

                         BILL
               No. We'll get off in Edinburgh
               and catch the next train back.

                         JOEL
               But of course, why didn't I think
               of that? Then maybe when we get
               back to King's Cross we can do it
               all again.

                         BILL
               Could we do that you think, on
               the same tickets?

Bill takes laptop, Hustler magazine and the book 'The girl
with the dragon tattoo' from the bag. Hands book and
magazine to Joel.

                         JOEL
               What are these for?

                         BILL
               To shut you up.

Joel SLAMS the book down.

                         JOEL
               Stop treating me like a mushroom
               Bill. I know you want to help me
               but none of this makes sense.

Bill looks up from the laptop. Recants.

                         BILL
               OK spunk bubble, listen up. Great
               Western Rail offer free wifi in
               first class. Not only that, their
               service provider is located in
               Germany so their IP addresses are
               outside of the UK.

                         JOEL
               Why is that important?

                         BILL
               Hacking is illegal, so I don't
               want to be traced. Wifi on a
               train is totally anonymous.

                         JOEL
               Why Edinburgh?

                         BILL
               A long train journey with good
               wifi. I can get 10 hours
               uninterrupted hacking done.

(CONTINUED)

                         JOEL
          Or 20 if we do it twice?

                         BILL
          Nice one Einstein.

                         JOEL
          So what do I do for 10 hours?

Bill points at the magazine and book. Joel looks down.

                         JOEL
          Why Hustler?

                         BILL
          'Cos they didn't have a BBW mag.

Joel rolls his eyes, picks up the book.

36   INT. CHIC WEB DESIGN OFFICE - MORNING

Sally's sharply dressed, shows cleavage. Colin and TOMMY,
30's, tall, thin, geeky, shows Sally her new office.

                         COLIN
          This is Tommy, he's our in-house
          technical genius. If you need
          anything he's your man.

They clumsily shake hands. Tommy's hand lingers too long;
he can't keep his eyes off her breasts.

                         SALLY
          Have you installed PhotoShop?

                         TOMMY
          I've installed Adobe Creative
          Cloud. It's the dogs bollocks.

                         SALLY
          Yes, but is Photoshop on there?

                         TOMMY
          Yep, the latest version.

                         COLIN
          Thanks Tommy. We'll call you if
          we need any more help.

He leaves. Sally looks at Colin and starts to giggle.

                         COLIN
          He gets a little excited, but he
          knows his stuff.

Colin sidles up closer to Sally.

                                              (CONTINUED)

                         COLIN (CONT'D)
               Talking about getting excited.
               Shall we have lunch later?

                         SALLY
               Calm down big boy; there's plenty
               of time outside of work hours.

     Colin pecks her cheek, slaps her arse, leaves. Sally puts
     down her bag, sighs as she sits.

37   INT. FIRST CLASS CARRIAGE - DAY

     Joel's slumped, asleep. Empty coffee cups, empty sandwich
     cartons. Bill closes laptop, taps Joel's shoulder.

                         BILL
               Come on numb nuts, time to go.

     Joel raises his head, looks around.

                         JOEL
               Did you find him yet?

                         BILL
               Not yet. I'm currently in
               Croatia.

                         JOEL
               I thought we're going to
               Edinburgh?

                         BILL
               I've traced the email trail to a
               server in Croatia. I now need a
               back door into Debian.

                         JOEL
               Who's Debian?

                         BILL
               That's above your pay grade.
               Let's go.

                         JOEL
               What, to Croatia?

                         BILL
               No we're at Edinburgh. Time to
               get off the train.

     Joel grabs the book, heads off. Bill grabs Hustler.

38   INT. CHIC WEB DESIGN OFFICE - DAY

Tommy looks at Sally's breasts as she speaks to him.

                    SALLY
          It says I can't get Hotmail.

                    TOMMY
          We block Hotmail so people don't
          spend all day on it.

Colin joins them.

                    COLIN
          That's OK Tommy, you can allow
          Sally access to Hotmail.

                    TOMMY
          OK Mr Curtis, I'll give her
          executive access.

                    COLIN
          You do that.

Tommy skulks away.

                    SALLY
          Executive access. I thought I
          already had that.

                    COLIN
          Yes you do. I was thinking of
          planning an executive weekend
          break.

                    SALLY
          You mean like a dirty weekend?

                    COLIN
          I'll have a wash first.

                    SALLY
          Don't you think it will look a
          little strange.

                    COLIN
          What having a wash?

Sally becomes coy.

                    SALLY
          No. The hotel register. Sally
          Curtis?

                    COLIN
          It has a certain ring to it. But
          we can use Smith if you like.

(CONTINUED)

                         SALLY
              I prefer Jones.

                         COLIN
              OK Bridget. Jones it is.

                         SALLY
              It's a deal Colin. Firth.

39   INT. FIRST CLASS CARRIAGE - DAY

         More Red Bull, sandwich wrappers on the table. Joel's half
         way through the book. Bill's at the laptop. Suddenly jumps
         up arms aloft; screams.

                         BILL
              Back of the fucking net!

         He kicks a can of Red Bull in triumph. It's not empty and
         red sticky liquid goes everywhere, including Joel's face.

                         JOEL
              Have you found him?

                         BILL
              I know where Bilbo Baggins lives!

                         JOEL
              Who gives a shit about a hobbit?

                         BILL
              Bilbo Baggins is your spammer's
              handle. And guess what?

                         JOEL
              What?

                         BILL
              He only lives in fucking London!

                         JOEL
              Bugger me! You genius. What's his
              real name.

                         BILL
              Martin Chivers.

                         JOEL
              You're shitting me?

         Bill stops prancing about.

                         BILL
              What? You know him?

                                                        (CONTINUED)

                              JOEL
                    If it's the real Martin Chivers,
                    I know of him.

                              BILL
                    Who's the real Martin Chivers?

                              JOEL
                    He used to play centre forward
                    for Spurs. I fucking hate Spurs.

                              BILL
                    Well his address is in Wembley.

                              JOEL
                    You got his address?

Bill turns the laptop around to show a picture from the
driving license of Martin Chivers.

                              JOEL (CONT'D)
                    Well it's not THE Martin Chivers,
                    but I still fucking hate him.

Joel gets up to give Bill a hug in appreciation.

                              JOEL (CONT'D)
                    You fucking star.

                              BILL
                    Don't come too close, your face
                    looks like it's had a period.

                              JOEL
                    Fuck off Bill.

40   EXT. COUNTRY SPA HOTEL - EVENING

       A Porsche speeds down a long gravel drive to an ivy clad
       country house. Colin opens the door for Sally.

41   INT. RECEPTIONIST DESK - EVENING

       Colin signs the book: Bridget Jones and Colin Firth,
       winking at the receptionist, who politely smiles but looks
       Sally up and down. Sally forces a smile, uncomfortable.

42   INT. LARGE PLUSH SUITE - EVENING

       They enter -- champagne on ice -- a large bunch of flowers
       with a card attached. Sally opens it.

       CLOSE UP: WANT TO MAKE A HABIT OF THIS?

                                                        (CONTINUED)

Sally turns to Colin, opens her mouth about to speak...he
kisses her. She pushes him away.

                    COLIN
          Not the gratitude I expected. But
          hey, if I understood women, I'd
          get a Noble Peace prize.

                    SALLY
          It's not you. Things are just
          complicated at the moment.

                    COLIN
          Is it something from your past?
          Your ex?

                    SALLY
          Not at all. He's history.

Sally looks down awkwardly and embarrassed.

                    SALLY (CONT'D)
          It's more about the future.

                    COLIN
          There's no pressure here. Let's
          have fun and see where it goes.

                    SALLY
          I've missed my period, I think
          I'm pregnant.

                    COLIN
          BOOM and she makes the knockout.

Colin mockingly falls back into a chair as though being
punched.

                    SALLY
          There's no easy way to say it.

                    COLIN
          I can. It's impossible.

                    SALLY
          Don't you remember the morning
          after Barbarella's?

                    COLIN
          Yes, but it's still...

Sally puts a finger on his lips.

                    SALLY
          Shush. I don't want any decisions
          yet. It's a big thing, but
          something I've wanted all my
          life.

He tries to speak. Her finger back on his lips stops him.

                    SALLY (CONT'D)
          I am keeping the baby. How much
          you want to be part of it will be
          up to you. I'll accept whatever
          you decide.

He's unsure what to say, tries to begin a few times.
Finally shakes his head.

                    COLIN
          Lets open the champagne and
          celebrate before it gets warm.

                    SALLY
          I can't drink alcohol for the
          next 9 months. You must know
          that?

                    COLIN
          BOOM! Noble peace prize ripped
          out of his hands.

Colin fills the glass and downs it in one.

                    COLIN (CONT'D)
          Looks like a party between me and
          Mr Moet tonight then.

He fills another glass.

43   INT. JOEL'S HOUSE - EVENING

Joel washes Red Bull from his face. Bill in living room.

                    BILL (O.S)
          I still don't think you need to
          take a gun.

Joel walks back into the room drying his face.

                    JOEL
          He could be a maniac or
          terrorist. I'd feel safer if it's
          in my bag.

                    BILL
          Tell you what. I'll come along
          for moral support. Can't have
          this Op going south.

                    JOEL
          Sounds good to me. I'll leave the
          piece in the car.

                                        (CONTINUED)

                         BILL
               You'll leave it here. I ain't
               driving with a gun on board.

                         JOEL
               OK Captain, you win.

                         BILL
               Come on numb nuts, let's get this
               over with. We'll pop over to mine
               on the way.

                         JOEL
               You can't tell Sam about this.

                         BILL
               Of course not. We need to pick
               the video camera up don't we?

                         JOEL
               Oh yeah. I forgot.

                         BILL
                    (under his breath)
               You just can't get the staff
               nowadays.

Bill heads for the door. Joel follows but on the way picks
up the gun, puts it in his pocket.

44   INT. HACKER'S HOME - EVENING

North London flats. Bill and Joel outside number 33 --
Bill puts his ear to the door, hears music.

                         BILL
               Someone's home.

                         JOEL
               How we going to play this?

                         BILL
               Follow my lead.

                         JOEL
               What's your lead?

                         BILL
               No idea.

Bill RAPS hard on the door, shouts.

                         BILL (CONT'D)
               It's the police. We have a
               warrant. Open up.

Silence.

                                              (CONTINUED)

                    BILL (CONT'D)
          You have 5 seconds to open up or
          we'll ram the door. 1.2.3..

A mortise lock turns followed by three bolts. Door
squeezes open a crack, small eyes peer out.

                    HACKER
          Show me the warrant.

Bill pushes the door open into hacker's face -- small guy
falls backwards. Bill strolls in. Joel closes door.

                    BILL
          Thank you for inviting us in.

Living room's like mission control. Bill admires the room.

                    BILL (CONT'D)
          This is awesome.

Hacker holds his bloody nose.

                    HACKER
          You're not the police. You can't
          come in here without a warrant.

                    BILL
          You're right we're not the
          police, so we don't need a
          warrant.

                    HACKER
          Get out before I call the police.

                    BILL
          We're not staying long. If you
          co-operate we'll be gone in 15
          minutes.

                    JOEL
          I wouldn't argue with him. He's
          wanted by Interpol. (to Bill)
          Shall I put the kettle on?

Hacker confused. Bill takes a hammer from the rucksack,
without warning SMASHES it into a 27 inch Apple monitor.

                    HACKER
          No! What the fuck are you doing?

                    BILL
          Just needed your attention as
          we're short of time. So are you
          going to listen to my proposal?

                         HACKER
               What proposal?

Bill shows spam email -- Hacker quickly scans paper.

                         BILL
               I believe it's your handy work.

                         HACKER
               And? It's just fucking spam, if
               you don't like it just delete it.

                         BILL
               Not going to work. You see, my
               friend here has a very jealous
               wife who read this and thinks
               it's real. She is now divorcing
               the shit out of him.

                         HACKER
               I'm sorry about that but I can't
               see how I can help.

                         BILL
               That's the easy bit. We just want
               to video you admitting that you
               sent the spam email.

                         HACKER
               You have got to be joking.

                         BILL
               Not at all.

Bill raises the hammer over a computer monitor.

                         HACKER
               NO! Wait! OK. OK. But I need to
               disguise my face.

                         BILL
               That's better. Now sit down while
               I set the camera up.

45   INT. BEDROOM AT SPA HOTEL - MORNING

Sally and Colin have finished a hot session; lying back
smouldering in each others arms.

                         COLIN
               What if I said I'd be happy to be
               there for you and your baby?

                         SALLY
               Our baby. I'd be thrilled.

Sally turns over, leans on him and looks into his eyes.

                                              (CONTINUED)

                         SALLY
              We don't know each other, so
              maybe this won't last. But I need
              to be a mother and will do what
              it takes, with or without a man.

                         COLIN
              You certainly know what you want.

                         SALLY
              I do and want you to be part of
              this journey. But if you turn out
              to be a shit then I'm gone.

                         COLIN
              This is so unexpected. But if
              you'll have me in your life, I'll
              take a chance on you. As a Dutch
              band once said.

Sally moves up closer to him.

                         SALLY
              Is that a proposal?

                         COLIN
              Maybe.

                         SALLY
              Swedish.

                         COLIN
              Sorry what?

                         SALLY
              ABBA. They were Swedish, not
              Dutch.

She puts his hand on her breast. Smiles.

46   INT. BEDROOM AT SPA HOTEL - EVENING

Room service tray on the bed. Sally dipping chips. Colin
retrieves his trousers; fishes out a Yale key, hands it to
her.

                         SALLY
              What's that for?

                         COLIN
              My house.

                         SALLY
              You want me to have a spare?

                                                        (CONTINUED)

                    COLIN
          No I want it to be our house.

                    SALLY
          Are you sure?

                    COLIN
          If it don't work out, I'll change
          the locks.

                    SALLY
          If it don't work out, I'll
          fire-bomb your house.

                    COLIN
          It's insured.

                    SALLY
          When do you want me to move in?

                    COLIN
          Whenever you want.

Sally looks away in thought.

                    SALLY
          Would you help me pick up my
          things from my ex's place?

                    COLIN
          Do you want me to give him a good
          hiding at the same time?

                    SALLY
          No. I just want some moral
          support.

                    COLIN
          Can't you just go there when he's
          not there?

                    SALLY
          I gave the keys back. I also need
          to tell him it's definitely over.

                    COLIN
          It really is a new chapter for
          you.

Sally pats her stomach.

                    SALLY
          A new chapter for all of us.

They hug. Colin's smile turns to worry.

47   INT. SHAH BAGH RESTAURANT - EVENING

        Bill and Joel clink their pints of lager.

                        JOEL
                That was amazing! I thought you'd
                lost it when you smashed his
                monitor.

                        BILL
                I just followed my gut instinct.

                        JOEL
                He was terrified of you. And to
                be honest, so was I.

                        BILL
                I'm just glad he wasn't a 6 foot
                6 gym jockey with a bent nose.

        Bill gulps his beer.

                        JOEL
                D'you think he'll call the
                police?

                        BILL
                He's a hacker - They'll
                confiscate his computers. I
                suspect he's a lot of stuff that
                ain't totally legal.

                        JOEL
                I guess you're right.

                        BILL
                What you smiling at?

                        JOEL
                I can prove to Sally it was all a
                mistake. I can get my life back.

                        BILL
                I'll drink to that.

        They clink their glasses again.

                        JOEL
                You're a real friend Bill.

                        BILL
                I know. Fancy a 69?

                        JOEL
                You what?

                         BILL
               Chicken Biriyani. Number 69.

                         JOEL
                    (grinning widely)
               Fuck off Bill.

48   INT. JOEL'S HOUSE - BEDROOM - DAY

     Joel in bed. SNORES. Mobile RINGS -- sleepily grabs it.

                         SALLY
               Joel. We need to talk.

     Joel immediately springs up, wide awake.

                         JOEL
               Sally. Is that you?

                         SALLY
               Well it's not Amy...

                         JOEL
               Sally I can explain everything.

                         SALLY
               I'm sure you've managed to come
               up with a great story by now.

                         JOEL
               It's not a story, I have proof.

                         SALLY
               Whatever. I need to come round to
               get all my things.

                         JOEL
               Sure. No problem. When?

                         SALLY
               Two minutes. I am outside now.

                         JOEL
               That's short notice. I'm not..

     Sally has hung up - he presses speed dial 2.

49   INT. BILL'S BEDROOM - CONTINUOUS - DAY

     Another mobile rings, 'Joel' on display. Bill answers.

                         BILL
               Yes numb nuts?

                                                        (CONTINUED)

                         JOEL (V.O)
                    She's here.

                         BILL
                    Who?

                         JOEL (V.O)
                    Who do YOU think?

                         BILL
                    The Queen's Mother?

                         JOEL (V.O)
                    She's dead.

                         BILL
                    How did she call?

Joel hangs up in despair.

50   INT. JOEL'S HOUSE - BEDROOM - DAY

      He jumps out of the bed totally naked, trips over his
      rucksack, falls flat on his face, bloodying his nose.

51   EXT. JOEL'S HOUSE - OUTSIDE - DAY

      Sally out of Colin's BMW clutching 'bags for life'.

                         SALLY
                    Hopefully this wont take long.

                         COLIN
                    Are you sure you don't want me to
                    come in?

                         SALLY
                    Better he hears this from me.
                    I'll ring if it gets too awkward.

      She holds her mobile up and heads for the gate.

52   EXT. JOELS - HOUSE FRONT DOOR - DAY

      Sally knocks on the door. Miss Franklin's in her garden.
      She waves. Sally forces a smile. The door opens -- Joel's
      stark naked, towel to his bleeding nose. Sally looks at
      his nose, his dick, then nose.

                         SALLY
                    You're a bloody mess.

                                              (CONTINUED)

                         JOEL
                    (through towel)
               I fell over.

                         SALLY
               Clumsy as ever. Can I come in or
               are you flashing Princess Shrek
               next door?

Joel peers past Sally, sees Miss Franklin waving at him.

                         JOEL
               Fuck. Come in, quickly.

                         SALLY
               I thought you'd never ask.

53   INT. JOEL'S HOUSE - KITCHEN - DAY

     Joel leads Sally into the kitchen. He opens the washing
     machine, takes out a dirty Arsenal kit and puts it on.

                         SALLY
               Bloody typical. An Arsenal kit.

                         JOEL
               Well a lot of my wardrobe was
               destroyed. Remember?

                         SALLY
               If you'd been around I'd have
               castrated you.

                         JOEL
               If you'd waited for the truth,
               we'd still be together.

                         SALLY
               Look. I didn't come here to
               fight.

                         JOEL
               So what did you come here for?

                         SALLY
               My things.

                         JOEL
               I understand how you feel and
               don't blame you for anything
               you've done.

                         SALLY
               How magnanimous of you.

                                                      (CONTINUED)

                    JOEL
          If you give me just 5 minutes to
          explain and you're still not
          happy then I will leave it be.

                    SALLY
          Five minutes?

                    JOEL
          Five minutes.

Sally sits, takes iphone out, sets the timer.

                    JOEL
          Shall I make us a cup of tea?

                    SALLY
          Joel you've got 5 minutes, this
          isn't a social visit. If you
          waste 2 minutes making a cup of
          tea, that's your decision.

                    JOEL
          Right.

Joel rushes out of the room.

                    SALLY
          What now?

Sally waits. Joel's back, with video camera, puts it on
the table, viewfinder facing Sally -- the battery's DEAD.

                    JOEL
          Shit.

Joel rushes out again. Sally shouts after him.

                    SALLY
          4 minutes left. And I have no
          idea what you are doing but I
          won't watch porn or football.

Joel back with power supply, too short to reach camera.
Scrapes table across floor, nearly knocks Sally over.
Finally connects camera, presses rewind.

                    SALLY
          Joel, what's going on? Nothing
          you show me will change my mind.

                    JOEL
          This will explain everything
          better than I can.

                    SALLY
          You've got 3 minutes.

Tape stops rewind. He presses play. First few frames are
of Bill doing a moony to test camera. Sally gets up.

                    SALLY
          That's it, I've had enough.

                    JOEL
          Wait. We were just testing the
          camera. Look!

Sally sees the hacker in the stupid disguise holding the
offending email, which the camera zooms in on.

                    HACKER
          Hello Sally. My name is Bilbo
          Baggins...well it's not really,
          that's just my hacking handle.

From left frame Bill swats the hacker with a newspaper.

                    BILL
          Get on with it.

Camera closes in and the hacker becomes more serious.

                    HACKER
          It was me who sent this email to
          Joel.

DING DONG, DING DONG; door bell nearly explodes.

54   EXT. JOEL'S HOUSE - OUTSIDE - DAY

Bill at door when Miss Franklin calls him.

                    MISS FRANKLIN
          Mr Foxy. How did my Babystation
          audition go? Do they like me?

                    BILL
          Oh hi Munchkin. I haven't
          finished editing it yet.

                    MISS FRANKLIN
          Oh. I thought I could start work
          soon.

                    BILL
          These things take time.

                    MISS FRANKLIN
          Okie Dokie. How about you come in
          for a cup of tea, cheeky boy?

                                              (CONTINUED)

                         BILL
               That would be great. But I need
               to see Joel urgently and then I
               have to pick my wife up.

                         MISS FRANKLIN
               Your wife? You didn't tell me you
               were married?

                         BILL
               You didn't ask.

Bill presses bell urgently - DING DONG DING DONG DING...

                         MISS FRANKLIN
               You lead me down the garden path.

                         BILL
               I can come by tomorrow and take
               more footage.

                         MISS FRANKLIN
               Fuck off. You weasel.

Miss Franklin hurls a rock at Bill, who ducks, just as
Joel opens the door, it hits him in the face. Bill shoves
Joel inside, shuts door.

55   INT. JOEL'S HOUSE - HALL WAY - DAY

Joel goes flying across the hallway as Bill rushes in.

                         BILL
               Sorry mate. That lunatic next
               door started hurling rocks at me.

Joel gets up, red faced.

                         JOEL
               Have I got a target on my face?

Bill looks closely at Joel's face.

                         BILL
               No. But you look fuck ugly today.

                         JOEL
               Fuck off Bill.

Bill ignores him.

                         BILL
               Is she here yet?

Joel ushers Bill into the front room.

                                                    (CONTINUED)

                    JOEL
          Yes. She's watching the video.

                    BILL
          Excellent. Looks like you're up
          for that excellent shag again.

Before Joel can answer, Sally comes out.

                    SALLY
          What excellent shag?

                    BILL
          He says you're an excellent shag.

                    JOEL
          Ignore him. He's full of shit.

                    SALLY
          You're both full of shit. I'll
          say this once Joel. I never want
          to see you again. I would
          appreciate it if you and fuckwit
          leave now and give me 10 minutes
          to pack my stuff.

                    JOEL
          You've just seen the video. It
          proves my innocence.

                    SALLY
          How do I know it's not a set up?

                    BILL
          I can witness it's genuine.

                    SALLY
          Since when has anyone taken you
          seriously? In fact, if you're
          involved I'm even more sceptical.

                    JOEL
          Look Sal, give me one more
          chance. I can take you to the
          hacker personally and he can
          explain to you himself.

                    SALLY
          Look Joel. Even if this were true
          it's too late. I've met someone.

Joel looks like he has been hit with a cricket bat.

                    SALLY (CONT'D)
          What's more...and I wasn't going
          to tell anyone this. I am
          expecting his child.

                                              (CONTINUED)

Joel crumbles. He is too cut up to speak. Bill takes Joel and leads him to the door. He turns to speak to Sally.

> BILL
> I used to fancy you, but you're
> just a heartless bitch.

Bill and Joel leave. Bill SLAMS the door.

56   EXT. JOEL'S HOUSE - OUTSIDE DAY

Joel and Bill mope down the path; only to be hit by a barrage of stones being hurled by Miss Franklin.

> MISS FRANKLIN
> You cheating bastard.

> JOEL
> I didn't cheat on her.

> MISS FRANKLIN
> Not you. That lanky piece of shit
> behind you who's the cheat.

Miss Franklin tries to get to Bill, there's a scuffle. In the end Joel pushes them both apart, screams at them.

> JOEL
> Stop it. You're both fucking
> idiots.
>   (to Bill)
> You're an idiot for not keeping
> your dick in your pants.
>   (to Franklin)
> And you shouldn't be flashing
> your tits and nasty underwear at
> everyone. What do you expect?

Miss Franklin pulls cardigan across cleavage, stomps off.

> BILL
> Fuck me Joel. You put her in her
> place. That was brilliant!

Joel ignores him, strides out the gate. Bill bewildered. Colin's BMW's at the curb. On the back window's a Tottenham Hotspurs sticker. Joel kicks the back wing.

> JOEL
> Wanker!

Bill gets to the car just as Colin gets out. Colin raises his hand towards the disappearing Joel.

> COLIN
> Oi! Come back here.

> BILL
> Not a wise move mate. He's mega
> pissed off.

Colin inspects the dent in the wing and turns to Bill.

> COLIN
> The cunt kicked my car.

> BILL
> Better than kicking your face. He
> hates Spurs fans.

> COLIN
> I'm going to call the police.

Colin gets his mobile out.

> BILL
> That's not a wise move.

> COLIN
> Why not?

> BILL
> I'm the only witness and who
> knows what I'm going to say?

> COLIN
> What can you say that will make a
> difference?

> BILL
> I don't know. I could say you're
> gay and had your cock out,
> flashed my mate and he hit your
> car instead of you?

> COLIN
> Don't be so fucking stupid. I
> have a girlfriend that can
> confirm I'm not gay.

Colin points towards Joel's house. Bill turns and it
clicks. He turns back to face Colin.

> BILL
> Tell you what. When he's calmed
> down, I'll have a word. Give me
> your details and I'll see if I
> can get it sorted.

                         COLIN
               That sounds more reasonable.

Colin gets his wallet out, hands a business card.

                         COLIN
               If I don't hear from him, how do
               I contact you?

                         BILL
               Oh. That's not a problem.

Bill throws his thumb in the direction of Joel's house.

                         BILL (CONT'D)
               Just ask Sally to contact me. My
               name's Bill.

57   INT. PUBLIC HOUSE - EVENING

Bill's at a table, noisy pub. Closing time. Empty beer
glasses on table. Joel, DRUNK, struggles with a full tray,
nearly loses the lot but Bill saves the day and tray.

                         LANDLORD (O.S.)
               Last orders.

He peels a bell LOUDLY

                         BILL
               Who the fuck are all these shots
               for?

                         JOEL
               They're for the cunts.

                         BILL
               What cunts?

Joel holds a shot of whiskey to the air.

                         JOEL
               Here's to Sally. Cunt.

He knocks it back, takes a swig of beer. His head drops as
though he's fallen asleep. Then with a jolt his head
shoots back up, takes another shot.

                         JOEL
               Here's to the Spurs wanker in the
               BMW. What's his name?

                         BILL
               Colin.

                                                        (CONTINUED)

                         JOEL
               To Colin. Cunt.

Same procedure as before.

                         JOEL
               Here's to Miss Franklin. Cunt.

Bill takes his coke and clinks the shot glass.

                         BILL
               Big cunt.

                         JOEL
               Go on Bill have a drink.

                         BILL
               Somebody needs to stay sober to
               get you home.

                         JOEL
               I ain't going home.

Joel's head bangs down on the table THUD. Passed out?

                         BILL
               Shit. Well at least you'll be
               easier to carry.

Suddenly Joel's head shoots up, Blood trickles from his
nose. He grabs a shot glass.

                         JOEL
               To Miss Spencer. Cunt.

Same procedure as before; as he is swigs his beer a burly
patron pushes past, accidentally bumps him, knocking beer.

                         BURLY PATRON
               Sorry Gov. My bad.

Joel jumps up and faces the large man.

                         JOEL
               Fuck off you ugly cunt.

                         BILL
               Calm down Joel.

                         BURLY PATRON
               Tell your girlfriend to behave. I
               apologized. His next mouthful
               will include my knuckles.

                         JOEL
               Try it cunt face.

                                              (CONTINUED)

Patron issues a right hook straight to the middle of
Joel's face. CRACK goes Joel nose, teeth. He's lifted off
the ground, flies across a table of drinks; liquid, glass
flies everywhere. Joel lands in a clump - Out cold.

                    BURLY PATRON
                  (turning to Bill)
            You fancy a knuckle sandwich?

                    BILL
            No thanks I'm on a diet.

The patron steps towards Bill. Bill raises his hands in
defence. Friends pull the patron away from the scene.

                    MATE
            They ain't worth doing more time
            for. Come on Spud, let's split.

As quick as it started the fracas is over.

58   INT. A&E DEPARTMENT - NIGHT

Bill holds Joel down as a nurse sows some stitches into a
gash on Joel's forehead. His face is a bloody mess.

                    BILL
            Come on bellend, let the nice
            nurse stitch you up.

                    JOEL
            I don't want stitches. I want to
            look ugly.

                    NURSE
            Come on Mr Hancock, it'll be over
            in a minute.

                    JOEL
            Fuck off bitch.

Bill puts a hand over Joel's mouth, uses all his strength
to hold him still.

                    BILL
            Sorry about this. It's been the
            worst day of his life.

                    NURSE
            Don't try to excuse him. Another
            word and I'm calling the police.

                    BILL
            Don't worry. I'll keep him under
            control. What time does your
            shift finish?

She finishes stitches, roughly puts gauze on the wound.

                    NURSE
          Get him the hell out of here.

                    BILL
          Yes ma'am.

SWISH of curtains -- she's gone.

59   INT. JOEL'S BEDROOM - NIGHT

Bill drags Joel up stairs, still drunk, cursing.

                    JOEL
          And Fletcher's a Nazi.

                    BILL
          Shut the fuck up.

Flower vase with a single flower. Joel throws out the
flower, raises vase like a shot glass.

                    JOEL
          To Paul Gascoigne. Cunt.

Joel downs the water, throws vase over his shoulder. Bill
grabs him by the collar, drags and dumps on bed.

Joel's already SNORING. Bill lifts Joel's legs onto bed.
He turns Joel on his side, packs pillow behind him.

                    BILL
          In case you throw up in your
          sleep buddy.

Bill looks at the mess of Joel's bloody bandaged face.

                    BILL (CONT'D)
          You're fucked mate. You don't
          deserve this.

Bill turns the light off, leaves.

60   INT. SCHOOL METALWORK ROOM - NEXT DAY

Bill reads porn mag hidden inside the Sun newspaper. Joel
limps in, face mashed up, cuts, stitches, plasters.

                    BILL
          You looking fucking awesome.

                    JOEL
          Thanks mate.

                         BILL
               Don't mention it.

                         JOEL
               No I mean it. Thanks for getting
               me home and sorting me out last
               night. I owe you.

                         BILL
               That's what friends are for. You
               got any naked pictures of Sally?

                         JOEL
               You what?

                         BILL
               You said you owe me. I was just
               thinking of what I'd like.

                         JOEL
               No I haven't got pictures of
               Sally. If I did you'd be the last
               person I'd show them to.

Bill shrugs, looks down at magazine, then looks at Joel.

                         BILL
               Who'd be the first?

                         JOEL
               The first what?

                         BILL
               The first person you would show
               them to?

                         JOEL
               Nobody. I ain't got no pictures.

Joel sees the porn mag.

                         JOEL (CONT'D)
               I don't believe you, looking at
               porn in school. That's desperate,
               even for you.

Joel spots letters for branding Sam's leather sitting in
margarine box; he absent-mindedly fiddles with them.

                         BILL
               I bet 11B ripped the piss out of
               you looking like that.

                         JOEL
               I ain't teaching today.

                                                       (CONTINUED)

                    BILL
          So why you here? I'd be down the
          pub. (beat) On second thoughts,
          maybe not in your case.

                    JOEL
          As there's only 2 days left of
          term, they said I should come
          back after Easter when 'my
          condition' has cleared up.
          They're treating me like a leper.

                    BILL
          We've all been there.

Joel spins round in a rage, rips into Bill.

                    JOEL
          Well I haven't. With Sally gone
          and no hope of fixing it, and
          this shit job in this shit
          school. I got no fucking idea
          what to do next.

Joel turns his back to hide his tears. He carries on
playing with the iron letters. He mumbles.

                    JOEL
          I should torch this place and
          then top myself.

Bill gets up and puts a hand on Joel's shoulder.

                    BILL
          I know how you feel mate. You'll
          get over it.

Joel shrugs Bills hand off, faces him, his tears roll.

                    JOEL
          You don't know how I feel. You
          haven't got a fucking clue.

Joel rushes from the room. Bill looks on, bewildered. On
the table the metal letters spell out SPAMMER, again.

61   INT. CHIC WEB DESIGN OFFICE - DAY

Sally at work. Tommy flirts with her.

                    SALLY
          It's my Hotmail; it's buggered.

Tommy sneaks a look at Sally's legs and short skirt. She
teasingly crosses them.

                                                  (CONTINUED)

                         SALLY (CONT'D)
               Can you un-bugger it?

                         TOMMY
               I'm an email expert. I've
               compiled my own sendmail daemon.

                         SALLY
               Whatever. Can you link my
               personal Hotmail with my work
               email?

                         TOMMY
               I can link your personal anything
               with anything you want.

                         SALLY
               Can't wait. Thank you Tommy. Or
               can I call you Tom?

From behind Tommy comes a voice.

                         COLIN
               Thank you Thomas. That'll do.

Colin walks over to Sally, pecks her on the cheek.

                         TOMMY
               Yes Mr Curtis.

Tommy leaving.

                         SALLY
               Thanks Tom.

She gives him a wink. Tommy blushes a retreat.

                         COLIN
               That was mean.

                         SALLY
               Yeah but if anything goes wrong,
               I have someone who will be
               desperate to fix it for me.

                         COLIN
               And what, as your boss, are you
               going to do for me?

Sally shimmies up her skirt, displays see-through panties.

                         COLIN
               You wicked minx.

Colin leans forward, kisses her on the lips.

62   EXT. SCHOOL - PLAYGROUND - NIGHT

        Midnight. Large pane glass window outside the metalwork
        room SMASHES as a house brick is hurled through it.

        A dark shadow climbs through and turns on a torch.

63   INT. SCHOOL - HEADMASTER'S STUDY - DAY

        Bill inspects fire damage in headmasters study. A pile of
        books, papers lie burnt in a corner.

                        BILL
                Kids.

                        HEADMASTER
                What do you mean Kids?

                        BILL
                Because they have no idea how to
                start a fire.

        Bill points at the pile of books.

                        BILL (CONT'D)
                If they'd stacked them to allow
                more airflow and used a little
                accelerant; then this place would
                have lit up like a Roman candle.

                        HEADMASTER
                You a closet arsonist then?

                        BILL
                I have to light the forge
                everyday in the metalwork room.
                You pay me to start fires.

        Headmaster throws two metal letters on his desk: J and U.

                        HEADMASTER
                These were found in the ashes.
                Know anything about them?

                        BILL
                So we are looking for a Nazi
                arsonist from Fletcher's class?

                        HEADMASTER
                What are you on about?

                        BILL
                Finding the letters JU in ashes.
                The last person to burn the Jews
                was Hitler.

                                        (CONTINUED)

> HEADMASTER
> Jew is spelt J-E-W not J-U.

> BILL
> That's why they must be from
> Fletcher's class; have you seen
> their spelling results?

> HEADMASTER
> Fuck off Bill.

Bill picks up the metal letters, walks out.

64   INT. SCHOOL METALWORK ROOM - DAY

Bill throws J and U into the empty margarine box. He
strolls over to the smashed window.

> BILL
> What the hell's going on inside
> your head Joel?

65   INT. HACKERS HOME - DAY

Joel hides in hallway outside hackers flat, carrying a
sports bag. Hacker's door opens, he walks out, turns to
lock the door, Joel rushes him; pushing him inside.

> HACKER
> What the fuck? Take it easy. What
> the fuck now? Where's your
> gorilla friend?

> JOEL
> I'm on my own.

> HACKER
> If you don't get out I'm calling
> the police.

Hacker pulls out mobile. Joel pulls the gun out.

> JOEL
> Not a good idea.

Hacker drops phone, raises hands, TERRIFIED.

> JOEL (CONT'D)
> It didn't work.

> HACKER
> Don't shoot. PLEASE! What didn't
> work?

                    JOEL
          The video.

                    HACKER
          I'm sorry. I'll tell her
          personally.

                    JOEL
          Also not going to work.

                    HACKER
          So what do you want me to do?

                    JOEL
          Nothing.

Before hacker can respond Joel SHOOTS him 3 times, his
face registers disbelief, falls to knees. Keels over DEAD.

66   INT. HACKER'S KITCHEN - DAY

Joel makes a cup of tea, humming to himself. An iron
contraption rests on the lit gas ring. Joel searches for
biscuits; finds a packet of value digestives, bites one,
holds a few in his gloved hands. Dangerously relaxed.

Goes to the gas stove, views contraption. Grasps it, walks
to living room. Hacker on floor, dead, blood pool, phone a
few feet away. Joel stands over him.

                    JOEL
          This won't hurt at all.

Joel thrusts branding iron on hackers forehead. A SIZZLING
sound, acrid smoke rises from BURNING flesh. He removes
branding iron, burnt in bloody flesh -- 'SPAMMER'.

                    JOEL
          Now that's what I call justice.

Joel picks up hacker's phone, dials '999'.

                    JOEL
          Yes. Police please.

Pops biscuit into his mouth, waits for police to answer.

                    JOEL (CONT'D)
          Listen up. There's a dead body at
          my feet.

                    POLICE
          Where are you?

Joel places phone on hacker's chest, without hanging up.

                                                   (CONTINUED)

                         JOEL
               Use GPS.

                         POLICE
               Hello. Hello. Are you still
               there?

Joel takes hacker's keys, calmly leaves, chomping biscuit.

67   INT. SHAH BAGH RESTAURANT - NIGHT

Joel walks in and is greeted by the same waiter.

                         WAITER
               Good evening sir. Will your
               friend be joining you?

                         JOEL
               Yes. He'll be here soon. I'll
               have a Cobra while I wait.

68   INT. SHAH BAGH RESTAURANT - LATER - NIGHT

Joel's alone. Three empty Cobra bottles in front of him.

                         WAITER
               It looks like your friend has
               standed you up.

                         JOEL
               Looks like it. Can I order a
               takeaway?

                         WAITER
               Most certainly.

69   EXT. SHAH BAGH RESTAURANT - LATER - NIGHT

Joel exits, takeaway in hand. Waiter holds door for him.

                         WAITER
               A good night sir. Come back soon.

                         JOEL
               You bet.

Joel walks 20 yards, dumps takeaway in public rubbish bin.

70   INT. JOEL'S BEDROOM - DAY

       Joel lying in bed snoring. Clock shows 08:45. Loud BANGING
       on his front door.

       Mobile rings. Joel slowly wakes, looks at the screen, sees
       it's Bill. Struggles out of bed, cursing in his y-fronts,
       heads downstairs.

71   EXT. JOEL'S FRONT DOOR - DAY

       Joel opens door. Bill punches him in the face, picks him
       up, man-handles him into a seat in living room.

                         BILL
                 Right fuck-face, why the hell did
                 you kill him?

       Joel touches his split, bleeding lip.

                         JOEL
                 Kill who?

       Bill raises his fist to Joel's face

                         BILL
                 Don't play innocent with me.

                         JOEL
                 Hit me again why don't you? It
                 won't change anything.

       Joel reaches for knife on the table, hands it to Bill.

                         JOEL
                 In fact let's cut the foreplay,
                 just kill me. I don't care.

       Bill's fist hovers. Their eyes lock. Bill relents, moves
       away from Joel, picks ashtray up, throws it at large
       ornate mirror above fireplace. SMASH.

                         JOEL
                 That's 7 years bad luck.

       Bill strides back and forth, finally sits down.

                         BILL
                 You used my letters.

                         JOEL
                 And?

                         BILL
                 That makes me an accomplice?

                                              (CONTINUED)

                         JOEL
               I stole them. It had nothing to
               do with you.

                         BILL
               I visited the hacker with you.
               What if my DNA is somewhere in
               his flat?

                         JOEL
               How will they know that?

                         BILL
               Because I know how the police
               work. They will interview
               everybody who knows you.

                         JOEL
               They need to catch me first.

                         BILL
               Where are the letters now?

Joel nods to the bag. Bill opens the bag.

                         BILL
               Fuck, they still got his bloody
               skin on.

                         JOEL
               What did you expect, marmalade?

Bill sits on the end of the sofa.

                         BILL
               It's only a matter of time before
               they find you and then by
               association, me.

                         JOEL
               They're never going to find me.

                         BILL
               Yeah right, you're such an
               experienced sleuth you can outwit
               the whole of the Metropolitan
               police force.

                         JOEL
               Actually I think I can. I may be
               a fool but I'm not an idiot.

                         BILL
               Great. Do tell. I can't wait to
               pick this apart.

Bill settles back into the sofa. Joel gets up.

                                                   (CONTINUED)

                         JOEL
               Fancy a cup of tea?

Bill incredulous, but can't see a reason not to.

                         BILL
               What the fuck. OK. You're a
               fucking nutter.

72   INT. JOEL'S HOUSE - LIVING ROOM - DAY

Joel finishes the story.

                         JOEL
               I then threw the curry in the
               rubbish bin and walked home.

                         BILL
               Where did you put the gloves?

                         JOEL
               Dropped them on a smelly tramp on
               the way home.

                         BILL
               Why did you walk, there is no one
               to corroborate that?

                         JOEL
               I made sure to walk close to CCTV
               cameras.

                         BILL
               What about the time-line? You
               were in the Indian after the
               murder happened; not at the time
               of the murder.

                         JOEL
               When I nicked his car, I drove
               like Billyo and was at the Shah
               Bagh within 15 mins of leaving
               his flat.

                         BILL
               Where did you leave the car?

                         JOEL
               20 meters from the restaurant,
               keys in the ignition. When I came
               out someone had stolen it.

                         BILL
               So they will assume whoever stole
               the car also killed him.

                                              (CONTINUED)

                    JOEL
          Yeah. I expect boy racers don't
          wear gloves. It's just not cool.

                    BILL
          How can you be so sure it would
          be boy racers?

                    JOEL
          A golf GTI with all the bling? It
          ain't going to be Granny Smith.

Bill tries to think of a challenge. He fails.

                    BILL
          You clever bastard. You may have
          pulled off the perfect murder.

                    JOEL
          Yeah, but where does it get me.

                    BILL
          Feeling smug inside. That's a
          powerful secret. A powerful
          secret empowers a man.

                    JOEL
          How would you know? Have you
          killed someone?

                    BILL
          I'm bloody starved. Got any grub?

Joel looks at Bill but doesn't push the point.

                    JOEL
          What do you fancy?

                    BILL
          Alphabet soup?

                    JOEL
          Funny ha ha.

                    BILL
          Bacon buttie.

                    JOEL
          Red sauce?

73   INT. JOEL KITCHEN - DAY

Joel fries bacon. Bill's drinks tea. Radio -- Talksport --
commentator talks about Spurs winning the night before.

                                              (CONTINUED)

                    JOEL
          Fucking lucky win. I hate Spurs.
          Maybe I should kill some Spurs
          players.

                    BILL
          Okay don't let it go to your
          head.

                    JOEL
          I only got one more to kill.

Bill nearly drops his tea.

                    BILL
          The fuck you have. Who?

                    JOEL
          Sally's new fella.

                    BILL
          Kill the father to a child you
          never had?

Joel slaps a plate with bacon butties down.

Radio announcer -- this mornings phone-in is about last
night's gruesome and unusual murder of a hacker.

                    BILL
          Wait. Listen.

Bill turns radio up.

                    ANNOUNCER
          Police have now confirmed that
          evidence at the murder victim's
          home supports the theory that he
          was in fact a serial spammer.
          Which leads on nicely to our
          phone in this morning. Is there
          ever a good reason to kill
          someone? Line 4, Tim from the
          Isle of Dogs.

                    TIM
          Spammers are the scourge of
          society. They should be put down.

                    ANNOUNCER
          That's a little harsh Tim. I
          thought estate agents or lawyers
          were the lowest of the low.

                    TIM
          I spend about 10 minutes every
          day deleting spam. That's over an
                    (MORE)

                                            (CONTINUED)

                         TIM (cont'd)
          hour a week, over 50 hours a
          year. So in 10 years a spammer
          has wasted 500 hours of my life.

                         ANNOUNCER
          Now you put it that way, I guess
          they're pretty deplorable. But to
          kill them and brand 'spammer'
          across their forehead? Good job
          he wasn't a gynecologist.

                         TIM
          Stunning calling card. Maximum
          respect to the killer. I hope he
          doesn't stop at one.

Joel turns radio off.

                         BILL
          Looks like you're going to be
          famous; like Jack the Ripper.

                         JOEL
          You helped. You tracked the
          spammer down and then made those
          bloody letters.

                         BILL
          Bloody letters. Very funny.

Bill pours more tomato ketchup on sandwich, wolfs it down.

74   INT. JOEL'S BEDROOM -FEW DAYS LATER - NIGHT

Joel SNORES. Mobile RINGS - grabs phone, mumbles.

                         JOEL
          I hope that's you Sally.

                         BILL
          Wake up numb nuts. Turn the TV
          on.

                         JOEL
          Bill?

Joel squints at the clock.

                         JOEL (CONT'D)
          It's half 2 in the morning. Why
          would I want to put the TV on?

                         BILL
          You ain't going to believe it. I
          think you've got away with it.

                                              (CONTINUED)

Joel shoots up in bed.

                    JOEL
          Has somebody else owned up to it?

                    BILL
          Better than that.

75   INT. JOEL'S HOUSE - LIVING ROOM - NIGHT

Joel wrapped in his duvet speaks to Bill on mobile. News
ticker bottom of the screen reads: BREAKING NEWS: Second
spammer murdered and branded.

                    JOEL
          How the fuck does this help me?

                    BILL (O.S)
          Wait! Here's the news bulletin.

                    NEWSCASTER
          This evening another Spammer,
          this time a woman, has been found
          dead and like last weeks murder,
          the word 'spammer' was branded on
          her forehead. The police have no
          suspects or clues at the moment.

                    JOEL
          Fuck Fuck fuck. What have I
          started?

                    BILL (O.S)
          You've started a revolution.
          You're a hero man!

                    JOEL
          Yeah, a hero with no name.

                    BILL (O.S)
          Does it matter? What's our next
          move?

                    JOEL
          You what?

                    BILL (O.S)
          How we going to capitalize on
          this?

                    JOEL
          Are you fucking mad? Last week
          you nearly throttled me when you
          knew I killed someone. Now you
          want to get on board?

                                              (CONTINUED)

                         BILL (O.S)
               Last week you were a prat. This
               week 'You Da Man!'

SILENCE.

                         BILL (CONT'D) (O.S.)
               Joel? You still there? Joel.

Joel sits dejected on the sofa.

                         JOEL
               It didn't get Sally back.

                         BILL (O.S)
               Don't give up on that yet pal. If
               it's meant to be it'll happen.

                         JOEL
               Yeah right.

Joel rubs his eyes. He glances over at the clock.

                         JOEL (CONT'D)
               It's fucking 3am. What the hell
               are you doing up anyway?

                         BILL (O.S)
               Babestation man.

                         JOEL
               But you've got a wife up in bed;
               is she still on a work to rule?

                         BILL (O.S.)
               No. She's on the rags.

                         JOEL
               Too much information Bill.

                         BILL (O.S)
               If you ask a question then you
               get an answer.

                         JOEL
               Don't you have any filter before
               the words come out of your mouth?

                         BILL (O.S)
               Nope.

                         JOEL
               Whatever. Anyway, what you got
               planned tomorrow?

                    BILL (O.S)
          Not much.

                    JOEL
          Fancy taking me down A&E?

                    BILL (O.S)
          Why? You about to cut your
          wrists?

                    JOEL
          Another example of your filter
          failure. No I need to have my
          stitches removed; they itch like
          hell.

                    BILL (O.S)
          Anything you want mate. I'm there
          for you.

                    JOEL
          I know Bill. You're a good
          friend. As weird as a 'Chocolate
          Potato', but heart in the right
          place. In fact you're my only
          friend.

Joel becomes a little emotional. He sniffs.

                    BILL (O.S)
          You blubbering? Pull it together
          man. You've committed the perfect
          murder and could be responsible
          for removing the worse human
          parasites. A&E? Why don't you go
          to your doctors?

                    JOEL
          It takes 2 hours to get through
          on the phone and then a 2 week
          wait for an appointment. Everyone
          goes to A&E nowadays.

                    BILL (O.S)
          Had no idea. I've not used a
          doctor since I was a kid.

                    JOEL
          Why ever not?

                    BILL (O.S)
          They keep computerized records. I
          like as little on file about me
          as possible. Besides, doctors
          give me hiccups.

                                        (CONTINUED)

CONTINUED: 85.

                         JOEL
               As I said 'Chocolate Potato'.

                              BILL (O.S)
               Joel?

                         JOEL
               What?

                              BILL (O.S)
               Fuck you.

                         JOEL
               Fuck you too. Good night buddy.

          Joel closes phone. Switches TV to Babestation.

76   INT. A&E OUTPATIENTS DEPARTMENT - DAY

          Joel and Bill wait. Bill reads the Daily Star.

                         JOEL
               I'm surprised you're not reading
               Hustler.

                         BILL
               Already read it and wanked myself
               empty.

          A woman in front looks around in disgust. Bill smiles and
          gives her a flirtive wave. She turns back, embarrassed.

                         JOEL
               I don't believe you sometimes.

          Before Bill can respond a nurse comes out.

                         NURSE
               Colin Curtis!

          Across the hall -- Colin stands, follows nurse.

                         BILL
               Fuck me.

          The woman in front looks around again.

                         BILL
               Not you dear, I've got some
               principles.

                         JOEL
               I've never seen any.

                                                          (CONTINUED)

                    BILL
          It's him.

                    JOEL
          It's who.

                    BILL
          Sally's new stud.

                    JOEL
          Where? Are you sure?

                    BILL
          100%. Wait here.

Bill gets up, follows Colin. Colin is ushered into a
cubicle, nurse pulls privacy curtain. Bill slips into next
cubicle, pulls curtain around, sidles up to the inner
curtain, listens to their conversation.

77   INT. HOSPITAL CUBICLE - DAY

Colin sits. Nurse looks through notes.

                    NURSE
          So Mr Curtis I see your vasectomy
          was carried out 3 years ago.

                    COLIN
          Yes. I thought I didn't want any
          more children.

                    NURSE
          And now things have changed?

                    COLIN
          Yes, I've met another woman,
          she's pregnant and I want to be
          the father.

                    NURSE
          Not yours then; unless this new
          woman comes from Bethlehem.

                    COLIN
          She doesn't know I shoot blanks.

                    NURSE
          So now you want to shoot live
          rounds, so she thinks it's your
          child?

                    COLIN
          It's not like that. I may want my
          own child with her.

                                              (CONTINUED)

                         NURSE
          Not my concern. I need to let you
          know that there is only a 60%
          success rate with a reversal.

                         COLIN
          I'll take it.

                         NURSE
          Pull your trousers and pants
          down.

78   INT. HOSPITAL CUBICLE - DAY

       Bill's can't resist having a peep through the curtain --
       nurse pulls surgical gloves on, grabs Colin privates,
       gives them a rough inspection.

                         COLIN
          Ouch. That hurts.

                         NURSE
          Pull your trousers up. Everything
          seems functional, underwhelming,
          but functional.

       She picks up folder, waltzes out. Colin, trousers round
       his ankles, sees Bill peering through the curtain.

                         COLIN
          What the fuck. It's you!

                         BILL
          We can't go on meeting like this.

       Bill makes a swift exit.

79   INT. GREASY SPOON - DAY

       As usual Bill's plate is loaded. Joel has a cup of tea.

                         BILL
          So in a nutshell he can't have
          made Sally pregnant.

       Light bulb moment. Bing! Joel gets excited.

                         JOEL
          That makes sense. Do you remember
          the day I came in and moaned that
          Sally had virtually raped me?

                         BILL
          Haven't stopped thinking about
          it.

                                              (CONTINUED)

                         JOEL
          That must be the day I made her
          pregnant. (Louder) SHES PREGNANT
          WITH MY FUCKING BABY!

Joel jumps up and circles the table, like he scored for
Arsenal. Other patrons startled; waitress shakes her head.

                         BILL
          So besides having a bigger dick
          than Colin, you don't shoot
          blanks.

                         JOEL
          How do you know my cock's bigger
          than Colin's.

Waitress is interested, looks at Bill to answer

                         BILL
          I watched the nurse examine it.

                         JOEL
          So how do you know how big my
          cock is?

                         BILL
          When you are changing from squash
          I have a right nosy.

                         JOEL
          You look at my dick? Are you gay?

                         BILL
          If you don't want anyone to see
          your dick, cover it up.

                         JOEL
          I will from now on.

Waitress has been drawn in. Bill turns to her.

                         BILL
          It's OK darling. My cock is
          bigger than both of them. Want to
          have a look?

                         WAITRESS
          Another coffee big boy?

Joel excitedly calls Sally. After a moment he disconnects.

                         JOEL
          Shit! She's changed her number.

                         BILL
               Send her an email.

                         JOEL
               She's changed that too.

                         BILL
               No, to her new email address.

                         JOEL
               I don't have it.

                         BILL
               I do.

Bill gets Colin's card out.

                         JOEL
               Is that the wankers card?

                         BILL
               Yes, and based on the naming
               convention I know Sally's email
               address. Give me your phone.

Joel hands over the phone. Bill starts typing.

                         BILL
               My dearest darling Sally...

                         JOEL
               I would never say that. She would
               smell a rat. Start 'Hi Sal'.

                         BILL
                    (narrates as typing)
               Hi Sal. I really miss your tits.

Joel grabs the phone from Bill.

80   INT. CHIC WEB DESIGN OFFICE - DAY

Sally is at her computer when her mailbox pings.

'From: epicgoonerfan@hotmail.com'. Sally sighs but is
intrigued by the subject,'Cuckoo's egg'. She reads.

                         (V.O. BY JOEL)
               'Hi Sal. You're pregnant with my
               child, not Colin's. Confront him,
               ask for a paternity test. I can't
               make you love me, but I still
               want to be the father to our
               child. Joel.'

                         SALLY
               Is this another one of your
               tricks Joel?

In frustration she bangs the desk

                         SALLY (CONT'D)
               Shit! Shit! Shit!

A cough at the door. Tommy wears, tshirt: 'Mustang Sally'.

                         TOMMY
               Is there a problem Sally?

                         SALLY
               My ex has found my email address.
               I don't need this pressure right
               now.

                         TOMMY
               So you didn't give him your email
               address?

                         SALLY
               Hell no.

                         TOMMY
               That's technically called spam
               and there are laws against that.

                         SALLY
               Is there anything you can do
               about it, Tom?

                         TOMMY
               Hell yes. May I?

He points at her keyboard. She bats her lids.

                         SALLY
               Have at it.

                         TOMMY
               I'll put a stop to this.

Sally gets uncomfortable, goes to stop him.

                         SALLY
               Actually even though they're full
               of lies, there's some personal
               stuff in there.

                         TOMMY
               Discretion is my middle name.
               Before I forward the email I'll
               delete all the contents. All I
               need are the headers.

                                             (CONTINUED)

Sally moves to give him access, allows their legs to touch. Within a few keystrokes it's all over.

                    TOMMY (CONT'D)
          There you go.

                    SALLY
          As easy as that? Does that mean
          no more emails from my ex?

                    TOMMY
          I guarantee within 24 hours
          you'll never receive another
          email from this loser.

                    SALLY
          Thank you. I owe you.

                    TOMMY
          You bet.

He leaves with just a little less swagger than John Wayne.

                    SALLY (V.O. BY JOEL)
          You're pregnant with my child,
          not Colin's. Confront him.

She looks out of the window in thought.

                    SALLY
          Confront him. Fuck.

81   INT. CHIC WEB DESIGN OFFICE - DAY

Sally walks to Colin's PA, who Looks up as she approaches.

                    COLIN'S PA
          Hi Sally. How can I help you?

                    SALLY
          I was just wondering if I could
          have a few words with Colin.

                    COLIN'S PA
          Sorry Sal, he went
          to Bournemouth.

                    SALLY
          Oh. I didn't know he was out.

                    COLIN'S PA
          He rushed out - something about
          an unhappy client. If he calls
          I'll tell him you're after him.

                                              (CONTINUED)

                    SALLY
          No that's OK. It can wait.

Sally leaves. PA, bitchy smile, does a small hand pump.

82   INT. IMMACULATE COMPUTER ROOM - NIGHT

Hard Rock blasts out speakers. Tommy surrounded by dozens
of screens, computers, rapidly typing commands in 'putty'.
Numerous screens scroll; network searches. Screen abruptly
stops; 1 result 'epicgoonerfan@hotmail.com' is shown. All
Joel's details on screen.

                    TOMMY
          Bingo. Found you Mr Hancock. Your
          spamming days are over.

Tommy lifts a rug -- under a loose floor board gets a tool
bag, opens it - exposes branding iron with 'Spammer'.

83   INT. LOCAL PUB - NIGHT

Joel keeps looking at his phone. Bill rabbiting on.

                    BILL
          Do you know how much Rufinol
          costs now?

                    JOEL
                (distracted)
          Never had the need for it.

Bill takes out the bottle, holds it in front of Joel.

                    BILL
          Bloody 25 quid.

                    JOEL
          Who's it for? Sam?

                    BILL
          Don't be silly, I can mine that
          hole anytime I want.

                    JOEL
          Who then?

                    BILL
          Trade secret mate.

84   INT. COLIN'S HOUSE - NIGHT

Sally on sofa, skims a magazine, cup of tea in hand. Keys rattle the front door. She goes greets Colin in the hall.

                    COLIN
          Hi Hon. Sorry I'm late, M25 was a
          bitch.

                    SALLY
          No probs. You could have texted
          me while sitting in traffic.

                    COLIN
          True. Sorry darling. I was on a
          call with my mother; it's her
          birthday today and once she
          starts I just switch off. You OK?

                    SALLY
          Sure. Are you hungry?

                    COLIN
          Famished.

                    SALLY
          I'll get your dinner out. I ate
          earlier.

                    COLIN
          Oh! Couldn't you wait until I got
          back?

                    SALLY
          If I'd had known when that was I
          might have.

                    COLIN
          Are you sure you're all right?

                    SALLY
          Fine

Sally heads to kitchen.

85   EXT. JOEL'S HOUSE - OUTSIDE - NIGHT

Bill drops Joel off.

                    JOEL
          Thanks mate.

                    BILL
          No worries. That's what mates are
          for. Give me a call if there's
          any developments.

                         JOEL
               You got it. With any luck we'll
               be back together at the weekend.

                         BILL
               I can't mate, I'm busy.

                         JOEL
               Not you. Me and Sally.

                         BILL
               I was just winding you up.

                         JOEL
               Fuck off Bill.

                         BILL
               You bet.

Bill pulls away from the curb.

86   EXT. JOEL'S HOUSE - OUTSIDE - NIGHT

     Tommy in van - high-tech surveillance den, like in FBI
     films but with juvenile posters of Warcraft and Pokemon.

     4K webcam focused on Joel's house.

     On screen, Tommy sees Bill's car pull away from the curb.

                         TOMMY
               Game on boys and girls.

     Tommy packs equipment - branding tool, gloves, gun, downs
     a Red Bull in one. About to turn the screen off when
     Bill's car comes back into view.

                         TOMMY (CONT'D)
               What the fuck?

     Bill gets out of his car with flowers, wine. Looks up and
     down street, puts his hands down his trousers, gives a few
     tugs in readiness, walks down Miss Franklin's path.

87   INT. COLIN'S HOUSE - NIGHT

     Colin and Sally at kitchen table. Colin's eats dinner,
     Sally watches.

                         COLIN
               Are you sure you don't want some
               more? It tastes great.

                    SALLY
          No thanks, I ate mine about an
          hour ago.

                    COLIN
          Yeah sorry about that. I know I
          should have texted you. Sorry I
          just forgot.

                    SALLY
          Does that happen very often?

                    COLIN
          Does what happen very often?

                    SALLY
          You forgetting something?

                    COLIN
          Are you OK? You seem tense.

                    SALLY
          Me? No, I'm fine. You just
          continue eating the lovely supper
          I cooked you.

Colin takes another mouthful, weary.

                    SALLY
          I was thinking.

                    COLIN
          Yes.

                    SALLY
          After we have this baby, would
          you be interested in having more?

                    COLIN
          Of course. In fact I was going to
          speak to you about that. I would
          like us to have a big family.

                    SALLY
          You were going to speak to me
          about that? Hmm, that's a
          coincidence.

                    COLIN
          I guess so. This tastes great.

                    SALLY
          So how were you going to approach
          this subject? I mean this first
          one wasn't planned. It sort of
          just happened.

                                        (CONTINUED)

                    COLIN
          I must admit it came as a shock.
          I didn't...

                    SALLY
          Shock? Do you think it's a shock
          when two people fuck they make a
          child?

                    COLIN
          Of course not...

                    SALLY
          I mean, I don't remember you
          asking me if I was on the pill or
          anything like that.

                    COLIN
          I guess...

                    SALLY
          And I don't remember you pulling
          out a condom and offering any
          precautions.

                    COLIN
          Well I thought...

                    SALLY
          In fact I don't think you needed
          to think about it at all?

Colin drops his knife and fork, raises his voice.

                    COLIN
          You've obviously got some bee in
          your bonnet.

                    SALLY
          I may have a bee in my bonnet,
          but do you have lead in your
          pencil?

Sally glares down towards his crutch.

                    COLIN
          What the fuck do you mean?

                    SALLY
          Did you not take precautions
          because you didn't need to?
          Answer me straight Colin. Do you
          shoot blanks? Or is this
          something else you conveniently
          forgot to tell me?

He looks her straight in the eyes.

                                        (CONTINUED)

                              COLIN
                    I love you Sally.

                              SALLY
                    Blanks or loaded dick?

                              COLIN
                    Who told you?

                              SALLY
                    I fucking knew it. All men are
                    fucking liars and cheats.

Sally stands, flips the plate of food all over him.

                              COLIN
                    I can explain. I never said I was
                    the father. You just assumed.

Sally picks up her coat, keys, bag - which wait by door.

88   EXT. COLIN'S HOUSE - NIGHT

        Sally slams door, keys his car, storms into the street
        just as a taxi rounds the bend. Hails it, steps inside.

89   EXT. JOEL'S HOUSE - NIGHT

        Tommy gets out of van, bag in hand. It's now dark. He
        opens Joel's gate, heads towards the door.

90   INT. JOEL KITCHEN - NIGHT

        Joel is making dinner - a microwave number. He reads
        instructions, headphone music BLASTING.

91   EXT. JOEL'S FRONT DOOR - NIGHT

        Tommy approaches the front door, looks around before
        taking a screwdriver-like device to the Yale lock.

        A squeeze of the trigger, the door opens, Tommy creeps in
        just as a taxi pulls up outside.

92   INT. JOEL'S HALLWAY - NIGHT

        Tommy takes out gun fitted with silencer, sees light under
        kitchen door, dons a black and white Vendetta mask.

93   EXT. JOEL'S HOUSE - OUTSIDE - NIGHT

Sally's taxi pulls up outside. Pays driver, jumps out, trots down path, eager. She notices front door is open.

94   INT. JOEL'S KITCHEN - NIGHT

Tommy pushes kitchen door open, gun aimed. Joel is peeling the meal wrapper.

> TOMMY
> OK punk. Drop the box.

Joel doesn't hear - his music's LOUD. Tommy shots into the ceiling. Joel spins around . PANICS - flings meal into the air to raise his hands. Curry flies everywhere.

> TOMMY (CONT'D)
> Don't move..

Sally crashes into room, having tripped over Tommy's bag in hall, blunders head first into Tommy, knocks him over.

Tommy falls, gun goes off, shooting him between the eyes. He slumps to the ground DEAD.

Sally lands on the floor, dress akimbo, displaying lacy black underwear. Joel stunned - looks between the dead body of an intruder and Sally's sexy underwear.

> JOEL
> What the fuck. Are you OK? What
> are you doing here?

Sally looks at the body, then at curry in Joel's hair.

> SALLY
> Who the fuck is that? And what's
> that shit in your hair? Oh my
> god. Is he dead?

> JOEL
> I hope so. I think he was just
> about to shoot me.

Joel touches his hair to discover the curry.

> JOEL (CONT'D)
> Lemon curry?

> SALLY
> Why would he want to shoot you?

> JOEL
> I have no idea. But I think you
> just saved my life.

(CONTINUED)

                         SALLY
               And killed someone in the
               process. Oh fuck I'm fucked.

Sally removes mask, revealing Tommy.

                         SALLY
               Shit. Fuck. Fuck and fucking
               fuck. YOU FUCKING IDIOT!

                         JOEL
               Who me?

                         SALLY
               No stupid. Him.

She points at the body.

                         JOEL
               What you know him?

                         SALLY
               Not very well. He works in IT at
               my new job.

                         JOEL
               So why is he here?

                         SALLY
               I asked him to put a stop to the
               emails you have been sending me.
               I guess he must be this mad
               spammer killer that's been on the
               news. What were the fucking odds
               of that?

                         JOEL
               But he can't be.

                         SALLY
               Why not?

Joel's embarrassed. Looks down.

                         JOEL
               Because I'm the spammer killer.

                         SALLY
               Yeah right and I am Madonna's
               twin sister.

                         JOEL
               Seriously. After you rejected me
               I had nothing to live for. So I
               went back and shot the hacker.

                                                      (CONTINUED)

                         SALLY
               So the video was real? But why
               did you brand his face?

                         JOEL
               I got the idea from Bill.

                         SALLY
               So he's involved as well?

                         JOEL
               He was branding some leather.

She puts her hands up stop the story.

                         SALLY
               I don't want to know.

They both look around bewildered.

                         SALLY (CONT'D)
               Now what do we do now?

                         JOEL
               Cup of tea?

95   INT. JOEL'S KITCHEN - NIGHT

          Sally at kitchen table, cup of tea - biscuits.

                         SALLY
               Nothing like a cup of tea. So why
               did you kill the woman spammer?

                         JOEL
               I didn't. That was a copy cat
               killing.

                         SALLY
                    (pointing at Tommy)
               So that idiot is some sort of
               vigilante?

                         JOEL
               Must be; but would he kill for
               you?

                         SALLY
               He wanted to get into my pants.

                         JOEL
                    (under his breath)
               Doesn't everybody?

She takes a biscuit.

                                               (CONTINUED)

                         SALLY
               Well it's certainly getting some
               public interest.

                         JOEL
               What? Getting into your pants?

                         SALLY
               No. Killing spammers.

                         JOEL
               That's not why you are here.

                         SALLY
               You were right. Colin's not the
               father, you are.

Joel does a fist pump.

                         JOEL
               Back of the fucking net.

                         SALLY
               Looks like you are going to be a
               father. Can you handle that?

                         JOEL
               Are you offering me a second
               chance?

                         SALLY
               No I am giving you a final
               chance. But under one condition.

                         JOEL
               Anything. I will do anything to
               put us right.

Sally looks down at the dead body.

                         SALLY
               Get rid of the body. I don't want
               to give birth in jail.

                         JOEL
               Just like that?

                         SALLY
               If you're the man for me you can
               do anything. I'll make it worth
               it.

Sally starts to hitch her skirt.

                         JOEL
               Black lace. I know.

She looks at him, confused.

                                        (CONTINUED)

                         JOEL (CONT'D)
                No worries. I know who to call.

                         SALLY
                Ghostbusters?

                         JOEL
                No. Bill.

Joel retrieves his mobile. Engages speed-dial.

                         SALLY
                Brilliant. Just the person I was
                thinking of.

                         JOEL
                There's a lot you don't know
                about Bill.

We hear the mobile ringing.

                                                    MATCH CUT

96   INT. MISS FRANKLIN'S BEDROOM - NIGHT

Mobile continues to ring. Miss Franklin on her back, on
the bed, snoring. Through her raised knees we see
Babestation on the TV.

Bill's head rises from between her legs, face sodden,
answers mobile.

                         BILL
                Hello.

We hear Joel on the other end of the call.

                         JOEL (V.O)
                Bill. I need your help.

                         BILL
                I am kind of busy at the moment.
                Can it wait until tomorrow?

                         JOEL (V.O)
                Filling your face again?

                         BILL
                Kind of.

                         JOEL (V.O)
                It's an emergency. You're the
                only one I know who can fix it.

                                                    (CONTINUED)

                         BILL
               This is intriguing. Can you give
               me a clue?

                         JOEL (V.O)
               Not over the phone.

                         BILL
               How soon do you need me.

                         JOEL (V.O)
               Straight away. Then afterwards
               I'll treat you to all you can eat
               at the Shag Bag.

                         BILL
               On my way. Be there soon.

Bill abruptly turns the phone off.

He picks up Miss Franklin's huge white cotton panties and
dries his face. He goes to put them down but the scent of
them makes him put them into his jeans pocket.

97   INT. JOEL'S KITCHEN - CONTINUOUS - NIGHT

Joel frowns at phone after abrupt disconnection.

                         SALLY
               What did he say?

                         JOEL
               He said he'll be here soon.

                         SALLY
               How soon?

                         JOEL
               He didn't say.

Sally gets up and starts to remove Joel's belt.

                         SALLY
               Long enough for this?

Kisses him, undoes zip, eases jeans, pants over his hips.
Joel removes her blouse, unclips bra. Sally caresses his
growing dick. Joel's hand's inside her pants -- Bill
BURSTS into the kitchen.

                         BILL
               Excellent. Do I just watch, or
               can I have sloppy seconds?

Joel and Sally separate, pull their clothes on fast.

                                                       (CONTINUED)

                          JOEL
              Fucking hell Bill! Can't you
              knock?

                          BILL
              The door was already open.

                          SALLY
              How come you are here so quickly?

                          BILL
              Joel said it was an emergency and
              I should be as quick as possible.

                          SALLY
              Where on earth were you? Next
              door?

                          BILL
              Well as you mention it. Yes.

Joel slaps a palm to his head as it comes together.

                          JOEL
              The ruffie. Of course.

                          SALLY
              What with that old trollope
              Franklin?

                          JOEL
              Did your £25 investment work
              then?

                          BILL
              Did what it said on the tin. And
              if we hurry up I can go back for
              the second-half.

                          SALLY
              You're fucking the local ugly pug
              bike?

                          BILL
              Beauty is only skin deep. And
              there's plenty to go around.

                          SALLY
              I don't believe you Bill.

Bill notices the body, points.

                          BILL
              You guys planning a threesome?

                                              (CONTINUED)

                    SALLY
          No Bill, he's dead.

                    BILL
          And?

98   EXT. JOEL'S KITCHEN - NIGHT

Bill and Joel settled at the kitchen table. Sally hands
them mugs of tea.

                    BILL
          So this guy is the vigilante?

                    JOEL
          Would seem so.

Bill cocks his head towards Sally.

                    JOEL (CONT'D)
          It's OK. I've told Sally about my
          indiscretion.

                    BILL
          What, that you murdered someone
          in cold blood?

                    SALLY
          It's a mute point now that I've
          also just murdered someone.

                    JOEL
          It was an accident.

                    BILL
          So what do you want me to do,
          murder someone so I can join your
          little club?

                    JOEL
          No. We need to get rid of the
          body; something you've had
          experience with.

                    BILL
          What! You've told her about that
          as well?

Sally holds her hands up defensively.

                    SALLY
          I don't want to know. Once we've
          disposed of the body we are all
          accomplices and therefore
          criminals.

                         BILL
              Excellent.

Joel bangs his mug down on the table.

                         JOEL
              Try to be serious for a moment. I
              don't want to spend the next 20
              years in prison.

Bill looks at Sally's cleavage - Sudden light bulb moment.

                         BILL
              We can kill two breasts with one
              stone. I mean birds.

Bill gets up to the window, pulls aside curtain, looks up
and down the street.

                         BILL
              He obviously hasn't walked here.
              His car must be outside.

Bill spots the van.

                         BILL (CONT'D)
              I am guessing it's that van.

                         JOEL
              What if its not?

Bill frisks the body, finds keys, presses the key fob, the
lights of the van flash outside.

                         BILL
              Bingo.

Bill picks up the body in a fireman's lift - picks up
Tommy's bag and gun and heads for the door.

                         SALLY
              What if someone sees you.

                         BILL
              I'll kill them.

Bill smiles and heads out of the door.

99   INT. MISS FRANKLIN'S BEDROOM - NIGHT

Babestation between Miss Franklin's legs again. Same
mobile ring. Same soggy face rises, phone in hand.

                         BILL
              Your timing is impeccable!

                                            (CONTINUED)

                         JOEL (V.O)
            Did you do it?

                         BILL
            Of course?

                         JOEL (V.O)
            Anyone see you?

                         BILL
            No one.

                         JOEL (V.O)
            So what now?

                         BILL
            When I have finished here I'll
            drive the van to the Isle of
            Dogs. It will be stolen within
            the hour.

                         JOEL (V.O)
            Thanks Bill. I owe you. Again.

                         BILL
            Just a few photos mate.

                         JOEL (V.O)
            I've said before. I don't.....

100   INT. JOEL'S BEDROOM - CONTINUOUS - NIGHT

        Joel lies on the bed, disconnects call from Bill. Sally
        starts to undress, bends over, pulls her panties down.

        She displays her gorgeous bare arse in front of Joel and
        his mobile. CLICK!

101   EXT. LONDON SUBURBIA - MORNING

        Bright Spring morning; sun drenches neat terraced houses
        in comfortable London suburb.

        POSTMAN, grey beard and turban, approaches gate. Stops.
        Faces Miss Franklin on her step in a skimpy dressing gown,
        Yorkshire Terrier in her arms.

        Terrier looks at postman; starts to growl, bares teeth.

                         MISS FRANKLIN
            Shush Spicy. That is the very
            nice postman.

        Postman passes package wrapped in black plastic.

                                               (CONTINUED)

                         MISS FRANKLIN (CONT'D)
                    Thank you, my rabbit has arrived.

Postie quickly down path of next garden, looks at ground.

He pushes a single letter through a tight letterbox, which
BITES shut as the letter....

102   INT. JOEL'S HOUSE - CONTINUOUS - DAY

        ....comes floating through the door, onto the mat, just
        missing the cat.

        The cat SPRINGS up the stairs, into the master bedroom and
        under a large wooden bed.

        SNORING above. A foot hangs over the mattress.

        The Mickey Mouse adorned bedside clock CLICKS to 08:19.

        A hand reaches over to stop the alarm.

        Joel stands over Sally, holds breakfast tray. Sally's the
        source of the SNORING, lying on her back, naked pregnant
        bump in the air.

        Joel places tray down, sits on the bed, strokes her tum.

                         JOEL
                    (whispering)
                If you're a boy, then Bill. If a
                girl then Billy.

                         SALLY
                Fuck off Joel.

        Joel smiles as Sally reaches over and munches a piece of
        hot buttered toast.

Notes:

Notes:

Notes: